"[SecondWorld] is gripping, prop⸺⸺⸺⸺⸺⸺⸺⸺⸺⸺ pacing and lively characters. Robinson's punchy prose style will appeal to fans of Matthew Reilly's fast-paced, bigger-than-life thrillers, but this is in no way a knockoff. It's a fresh and satisfying thriller that should bring its author plenty of new fans."

—Booklist

"A brisk thriller with neatly timed action sequences, snappy dialogue and the ultimate sympathetic figure in a badly burned little girl with a fighting spirit... The Nazis are determined to have the last gruesome laugh in this efficient doomsday thriller."

— Kirkus Reviews

"Relentless pacing and numerous plot twists drive this compelling stand-alone from Robinson... Thriller fans and apocalyptic fiction aficionados alike will find this audaciously plotted novel enormously satisfying."

— Publisher's Weekly

"A harrowing, edge of your seat thriller told by a master storyteller, Jeremy Robinson's Secondworld is an amazing, globetrotting tale that will truly leave you breathless."

— Richard Doestch, bestselling author of HALF-PAST DAWN

"Robinson blends myth, science and terminal velocity action like no one else."

— Scott Sigler, NY Times bestselling author of NOCTURNAL

"Just when you think that 21st-century authors have come up with every possible way of destroying the world, along comes Jeremy Robinson."

— New Hampshire Magazine

PRAISE FOR THE JACK SIGLER THRILLERS

THRESHOLD

"Threshold elevates Robinson to the highest tier of over-the-top action authors and it delivers beyond the expectations even of his fans. The next Chess Team adventure cannot come fast enough."

— Booklist - Starred Review

"Video game on a page? Absolutely. Fast, furious unabashed fun? You bet."

— Publishers Weekly

"Jeremy Robinson's Threshold is one hell of a thriller, wildly imaginative and diabolical, which combines ancient legends and modern science into a non-stop action ride that will keep you turning the pages until the wee hours."

— Douglas Preston, NY Times bestselling author of IMPACT

"With Threshold Jeremy Robinson goes pedal to the metal into very dark territory. Fast-paced, action-packed and wonderfully creepy! Highly recommended!"

— Jonathan Maberry, NY Times bestselling author of
DUST & DECAY

"With his new entry in the Jack Sigler series, Jeremy Robinson plants his feet firmly on territory blazed by David Morrell and James Rollins. The perfect blend of mysticism and monsters, both human and otherwise, make Threshold as groundbreaking as it is riveting."

— Jon Land, NY Times bestselling author of
STRONG ENOUGH TO DIE

"Jeremy Robinson is the next James Rollins."

—Chris Kuzneski, NY Times bestselling author of
THE DEATH RELIC

"Jeremy Robinson's Threshold sets a blistering pace from the very first page and never lets up. For readers seeking a fun rip-roaring adventure, look no further."

— Boyd Morrison, bestselling author of
THE ROSWELL CONSPIRACY

INSTINCT

"If you like thrillers original, unpredictable and chock-full of action, you are going to love Jeremy Robinson's Chess Team. INSTINCT riveted me to my chair."

— Stephen Coonts, NY Times bestselling author of PIRATE ALLEY

I AM
COWBOY

JEREMY ROBINSON

ALSO BY JEREMY ROBINSON

Standalone Novels

SecondWorld
Project Nemesis
Island 731
I Am Cowboy

The Jack Sigler Novels

Prime
Pulse
Instinct
Threshold
Ragnarok
Omega

The Chess Team Novellas
(Chesspocalypse Series)

Callsign: King — Book 1
Callsign: Queen — Book 1
Callsign: Rook — Book 1
Callsign: King — Book 2
Callsign: Bishop — Book 1
Callsign: Knight — Book 1
Callsign: Deep Blue — Book 1
Callsign: King — Book 3

The Origins Editions
(First five novels)

The Didymus Contingency
Raising The Past
Beneath
Antarktos Rising
Kronos

The Last Hunter
(Antarktos Saga Series)

The Last Hunter — Descent
The Last Hunter — Pursuit
The Last Hunter — Ascent
The Last Hunter — Lament
The Last Hunter — Onslaught

Writing as Jeremy Bishop

Torment
The Sentinel
The Raven

I AM
COWBOY

1

The woman's voice, ragged from dehydration and hours of screaming, didn't carry far. Even before she'd been beaten and locked away, the hundred feet of soil, stone and sand above her head guaranteed that no one would hear her pleas for help. She was alone, and she knew it, but she'd be damned before letting the two guards standing outside her makeshift cell think she'd been defeated.

So she screamed. "Help! Someone help me!"

As the last echo of her gravelly cry faded from the small stone chamber, a sharp report exploded from the other side of the wooden door. It was quickly followed by a shout of pain and a second boom that shook dust from the ceiling and stung her ears. The twin blasts were followed by the sound of two bodies hitting the floor.

The woman pushed herself away from the door, gasping in surprise as it suddenly burst inward, wood splintering beneath the force of a powerful kick. Dust billowed into the space, lit by twin halogen lamps in the tunnel beyond. A figure stepped into the light, revealing the indistinct silhouette of a man.

As he stepped forward, over one of the dead guards, who was dressed like a tourist, the shape of her rescuer resolved. He was tall and slim. A revolver rested comfortably in each hand. But the most distinguishing feature was the Stetson hat resting atop his head. It struck her as unusual because it was a relatively unheard of accessory, not just in Tanis, Eygpt, which they were beneath, but in all of the Middle East—primarily because it was distinctly American.

But was he a friend? She held the secret to an ancient source of power for which several men, corporations or governments, might kill. This man could simply be after the same thing. "Why are you here?"

The man paused in the light, perhaps confused by the question.

"Heard screaming," he said, his accent Eastern European.

"What do you want?" she asked.

His head and Stetson tilted to the side, as though trying to comprehend her line of questioning. "To...rescue you?"

"*Before* you heard me," she explained. "Why were you here?"

"Ahh," the man says. She can't see it, but the woman is sure the man is grinning. "To kill Nazis."

Nazis.

Who would believe it? A year ago, she would have laughed at the idea, but it had been only six months since Nazis, plotting since the end of World War II, had nearly carried out a worldwide genocide. Their plan had been undone by a man the world knew as Lincoln Miller, who had survived the first attack that wiped out Miami. While many of the Nazis in charge had been killed or captured and their network destroyed, there were still hundreds of thousands of them around the world, running for cover, blending back into their lives, or as the case may be, searching for new ways to resurrect a long-dead war.

Given the fact that there were now two dead Nazis lying outside her door, she decided to believe him. She just had one last question. "Who are you?"

The man stepped forward and to the side, allowing the light to strike his side, revealing his smiling, stubble-covered face. He wore a tactical vest over a white shirt with rolled up sleeves, a red bandanna around his neck, blue jeans and a pair of dust covered, brown leather boots. He holstered his two revolvers, one on each hip. "I am Cowboy," he said. "I am gunslinger."

2

Milos Vesely, known to his friends and enemies simply as Cowboy, reached down and pulled the woman to her feet. She was nearly as tall as he was, and in his opinion, she was too fair a woman to be held in such dire conditions. When she rose fully into the light, the blood red split on her lip made him flinch. He reached out his hand, placed his fingers gently under her chin and turned her to fully see the bruising. "Who would do this to such beautiful woman?"

The woman grinned and then winced as the wound stretched. "You realize you spoke that aloud?"

He nodded. "Was serious. Who did this?"

She pointed behind Vesely, to the dead man in the doorway. "You've already avenged me."

"He is just guard," Vesely pointed out. "Not man in charge."

"I don't know who he is," the woman said. "But he had a thick German accent and struck me as...off."

"Old?" Vesely asked. "But not?"

"Yes!" the woman said. "Couldn't have been older than forty, but his mannerisms were old fashioned, in an angry German way. Who was he?"

Vesely shrugged. He didn't know the man's identity, only where he came from. "Would you believe cryogenically frozen Schutzstaffel thawed out and revived to help carry out SecondWorld?"

SecondWorld was the codename for what the planet would have become if the Nazi genocide had been seen through to fruition—a world where only pure Aryans would have survived. Given the woman's deeply tanned skin, almost black eyes and Middle Eastern features, Vesely knew that she would not have lived to see SecondWorld.

"I suppose I would," she said, surprising him. Despite the fact that the human race was nearly wiped out by a giant cloud of iron particles oxidizing in the atmosphere, removing the oxygen from the air, some people still had trouble believing the particulars of how the Nazis pulled it off.

"Now then," Vesely said, "Why are *you* here?"

"Shouldn't we be leaving?" she replied.

Vesely motioned to the door. "All dead. No rush."

"The others were coming back," she said.

Vesely tried to not show his surprise. He'd killed nine men in the tunnels above them. Most put up little fight, but he'd assumed they represented the entire force. He'd never found more than a handful of Nazis together at one time. They tended to stay spread out, organized like terrorist cells, so they couldn't all be caught in one location, like the thousands who died when SecondWorld was prevented at the secret underground base in Dulce, New Mexico. "How many?"

"I don't know," the woman said, starting to sound nervous. "I didn't see them all."

"Make guess."

She shrugged. "Fifty?"

"Hovno!" Vesely whispered.

"What?"

"I say 'shit' in Czech. Is curse."

"I know what shit means," she said.

Vesely drew a single revolver and headed for the door. "Come, we walk and talk."

Stepping over the dead guard and around a slowly growing pool of blood from the second, Vesely moved into the brightly lit stone tunnel.

The woman followed, grunting in disgust as she stepped past the bodies. "Geez," she said, looking down at the man whose head was partially missing. "What did you shoot them with?"

Holding up the revolver, he replied, "Is Smith & Wesson special edition revolver made for .38 Super ammunition. Only two hundred in world. Powerful and merciful."

"Merciful?" she asked, her voice full of doubt and muffled by her olive drab T-shirt, which she'd hoisted up over her mouth and nose.

"*Ano,*" he said and then translated, "yes". Slow death from small bullet is very painful. Quick death from .38 is—"

"I get it," the woman said. She slid up next to him at the tunnel's bend, which led to an ancient staircase carved into solid stone thousands of years previously, just like all the other tunnels in the subterranean labyrinth.

Vesely peeked around the corner. Lying on the stairs was the man he killed on his way in. "Come." He led her up the stairs, past the man whose adventurous-looking khaki vest was soaked with blood from a bullet wound over his heart.

At the top of the stairs, they reached a T-junction. Vesely paused, looked both ways and then started to the left, which would take them to another set of stairs and eventually back to the surface. As they walked cautiously onward, he asked. "Okay, now you tell. Who are you?"

The woman seemed reluctant to answer, but eventually said, "Dr. Sarah Pasha, and before you ask, my mother was Egyptian and my father was American."

"Interesting heritage," Vesely noted, stepping around another body.

"My father was an archeologist," she explained.

"Like you?" Vesely asked.

Pasha nodded. "How did you kill these men so silently? I only heard the two shots outside my cell."

Vesely turned around and patted the sound-suppressed Mark 23 SOCOM handgun holstered on the front of his body armor. "Was gift from Navy Seal friend."

"You have friends in the U.S. Navy?" she asked, dubious.

Vesely smiled, filling the grin with a thick dose of "you have no idea."

Feeling confident that they still had the tunnels to themselves—newcomers would have found the bodies outside and sounded the alarm—Vesely quickened his pace through the dimly lit tunnels and up the stairs. As they rose through the musty stairwell, the air grew warm and dry, accentuating the scent of hot metal and burnt chemicals lingering from his previous gunplay.

The final set of ancient stairs leading to the surface was dark, the external lights extinguished by Vesely when he first set upon the camp, blinding his enemy before ending their lives. He took the steps cautiously, leading with his revolver and holding his breath, so he could hear even the slightest noise. But it was a wasted effort. He could have heard the rumble of approaching trucks with his ears blocked.

The bright glow of headlights passed through the fabric of the white canvas tent covering the entrance. They didn't have long.

"Oh God," Pasha said, "They're here."

Vesely holstered his weapon and pulled a phone from his pocket, dialing a saved number.

"What are you doing?" she asked. "We need to go!"

Vesely shook his head. "We are trapped."

"Then we should go back."

"First call," Vesely said.

"Call who?"

"Back-up. Survivor."

The lights grew brighter. The vehicle's occupants were no doubt aware that something was amiss. The camp's halogen lamps had been shot out and the guards were no longer at their posts. It wouldn't be long before he had company, and if Pasha was right, Vesely didn't have enough bullets to kill all fifty men. They needed help.

"Survivor?" Pasha asked, panic reducing her voice to a near whisper. "What are you talking abou—"

"*The* Survivor," Vesely said, knowing it was all the explanation she would need.

"Lincoln Miller?"

Vesely nodded. "He is Navy Seal who gave gun. Was his. Reward for helping to save world."

"*You* were at Dulce?"

Vesely lowered the phone with a sigh. "Someday Cowboy will get movie deal and world will know whole story."

"What are you doing?" Pasha asked, looking at the lowered phone.

"No signal," Vesely said, pocketing the phone and drawing both revolvers. "You run fast?"

"What? No! You said we were trapped."

"When I thought back-up could come. Now, we fight our way out." Vesely gave a confident smile. "Do not worry. I told you, I am gunslinger. Stay close."

Vesely stepped into the tent and parted the entrance just a few inches.

Twenty men with automatic rifles and submachine guns stood waiting, weapons raised and aimed at him. With wide eyes, he glanced to the right and saw the man in charge. The man wore modern military garb, all black, but his slicked back hair style screamed mid-century Germany.

When the man met Vesely's gaze, his mouth snapped open, shouting a command "Schießen!" which Vesely knew was German for, "Shoot!"

3

Vesely dove backwards, grabbing Pasha around the waist and tackling her down the stone stairway, just as a stream of bullets tore through the tent and the stone entryway. They fell in a heap of tangled limbs, rolling down the fifteen stone steps. Each impact drove into him like a hard punch, and by the time they reached the dusty stone hallway, Vesely felt as though he'd fought a round in the UFC. He coughed as he landed flat on his back. There was barely enough air in his lungs to whisper, "Cover ears!"

But Pasha heard the command just in time, raising her hands as Vesely's revolver came up. Just as the flesh of her palms compressed over her ears, the trigger squeezed back, and the weapon filled the tunnel with the sound of thunder.

A man at the top of the stairs snapped back, his head turned up toward the tent's ceiling, which was now marred with his brain matter. He toppled over backwards to be replaced by a second man. Vesely dispatched him with the same lethal accuracy. These men were either undisciplined or extremely fanatic. And both possibilities were bad news, because if they kept pouring in, Vesely would run out of ammunition before they ran out of men.

Happily, the third man in line ducked back, repelled by the face full of blood and gore he received from the second man.

The harsh words of angry Germans rolled down the tunnel, as Pasha got to her feet and helped Vesely up. He crouched down in a shooter's stance, keeping his aim toward the top of the stairs.

"What are you doing?" Pasha asked.

"Is bottleneck," he replied. "I don't have enough ammunition to kill them, but they don't know that. Next who shows face, I kill. And again. Until they give up."

"They *won't* give up," she said with a confidence that made Vesely risk a glance in her direction.

"Why not?"

"Because they know what's down—"

"Kovboj, is that you?" a deep German accented voice called down the stairs, the speaker keeping well out of sight.

"Hovno!" Vesely muttered.

"I wish you'd stop saying that," Pasha said.

"Is Dr. Oskar Dirlewanger," Vesely whispered, hoping the fear in his voice wouldn't reach the man just out of view at the top of the stairs. "Is Sturmbannführer. A Major."

"That doesn't mean anything to—"

"Kovboj, when will your thirst for German blood be quenched?" Dirlewanger asked, a hint of mockery decorating his words.

"Is not German blood I seek to spill," Vesely shouted back. "Is Nazi blood!" He punctuated the statement by firing off a shot. He was pleased to hear several men dive to the floor with shouts of surprise.

But not Dirlewanger. He laughed. "Oh, Kovboj, had I an adversary like you during the war, I might not have elected to be frozen. I will give you a moment to consider your options, or perhaps to say your goodbyes."

"We need to get out of here," Vesely whispered to Pasha.

"What happened to the bottleneck theory?"

"Will not work," Vesely said. "Will explain later."

"But where will we go?" Pasha asked.

It was a good question, but Vesely suspected she already had the answer. "Dirlewanger is smart man. Would not expose himself without cause." He squinted at her. "Is secret tunnel, yes?"

She frowned.

Confirmation enough.

"You can open?"

She sighed, once again confirming without words.

"You lead way. I cover."

Pasha looked unhappy about this, and Vesely unders-tood that she was actually be more concerned about protecting whatever ancient relics lay beneath them, or even the power source of which she had spoken. No matter how noble her cause was, it no longer mattered. "If we are killed, they will still find way in, but not with brains. With bombs."

A metallic clacking sound drew their eyes to the stairway. A green fragmentation grenade tumbled toward them, bouncing off the flat stone steps. While Pasha turned and ran, Vesely leaned into the stairway, reached out and caught the grenade, hoping that the man who'd lobbed it down the stairs hadn't let it 'cook' by holding it for a few seconds after pulling the pin.

With a snap of his wrist, Vesely sent the grenade sail-ing back up the steps. He dove in the opposite direction, covering his head with his arms and opening his mouth to prevent the pressure wave from rupturing his lungs and drowning him in his own blood.

The grenade exploded in the stairway just 1.5 seconds after Vesely released it. Although he was protected from the metal fragments, the shockwave still stabbed his ears and knocked the wind out of him. As his mind and body reeled from the impact, some part of him kept screaming to move. His legs were in motion even before he got back to his feet.

He stumbled back, away from the stairs, clinging to the wall for balance.

From the stairs above came Dirlewanger's voice. "Angreifen! Angreifen! Angreifen!"

Attack! Attack! Attack!

Milos Vesely had lived through what was nearly the end of the world, fighting off neo-Nazis and resurrected Nazis, not to mention killer robotic drones. But none of that frightened him as much as Dirlewanger. Not because the man was dangerous, but because the man was twisted. He might just kill Vesely. But Pasha? Dirlewanger had a history of entertaining his men by force-feeding strychnine to female prisoners and watching them die painfully. But even worse, the sinister doctor was tame compared to the men he led, the dreaded SS Dirlewanger Brigade.

As an army of boots descended the stone stairway, Vesely did the only thing he *could* do. He turned and fled, hoping that whatever secret exit Pasha knew about could be opened and closed, in seconds. If not, they were both dead. Worse, if there was some kind of ancient super weapon hidden beneath the ground, their failure might make SecondWorld a reality once more.

4

As Vesely approached the T-junction, he looked for signs of Pasha's retreat and found nothing. There were no fresh scuff marks. There was no way to tell whether she headed right, back toward the cell or straight. And there was no time to make the wrong choice.

"Pasha!" Vesely shouted. "Which way?"

A gun fired behind him, making him cringe and duck. His ears already ached from the shooting earlier. Now, each shot felt like a needle being jabbed into his eardrum. A bullet pinged off the stone wall above his head, just missing his Stetson.

He was about to call out for Pasha again, but her voice reached him first. "Here!"

Vesely turned right, slipping on the smooth, dusty floor. He slid like a baseball player stealing second, and struck the wall. His leg throbbed from the impact, but the fall saved him from another bullet that buried itself in the ancient wall. Scrambling to his feet, Vesely charged through the passage until he finally saw Pasha ahead. She was on her hands and knees, scratching at the floor.

"What are you doing?" Vesely asked, out of breath. She ignored his question, dragging the butt of one of the dead guard's guns across the floor, leaving an arced scratch behind.

"Where is door?" Vesely asked, taking Pasha by the arm and yanking her to her feet.

"Hey!" she shouted. She pulled her arm from his grasp, but the sound of approaching boots stifled her complaint.

"This way!" she said. She ducked back into the dark recesses of the room that had been her prison.

Before following her, Vesely took the one remaining gun from the second dead guard. Between him and Pasha, they now had five weapons. Not bad, though not exactly good against fifty-odd killers.

"Back here," Pasha said from the shadows. She knelt in the corner, lifting up a two foot square slab of stone, one of many tiles that made up the room's floor. Vesely helped her raise the stone higher, revealing an empty black hole beneath.

"It's a five foot drop to a sloped tunnel," Pasha said.

Vesely gave a nod. "Go first."

Pasha lowered her legs into the open space, preparing to drop down.

The sound of approaching boots slowed to a stop.

"Pasha," said a voice, almost gently. "Are you there?"

Vesely turned to Pasha, who had frozen in place over the hidden tunnel. He whispered, "You know voice?"

Pasha nodded.

"Pasha," the man said, calmly, like they were having a conversation over breakfast. "You were never supposed to be hurt. The men who were watching you got...carried away."

Pasha opened her mouth to reply, but Vesely placed a hand against her lips, shook his head, no, and gave her a grim stare that let her know only death would follow her words. She clamped her mouth shut.

"If you can hear me, Pasha... If you're in there... The man you're with now? He's the dangerous one. He's the killer."

Vesely motioned for the hole, asking for her trust, and she agreed. She disappeared into the dark.

Hushed voices spoke in German as Vesely lowered himself into the hole. His feet reached the bottom quickly, and he ducked inside, carefully lowering the two inch-thick square tile down above his head.

"We're coming in Pasha," the man said. "Please don't shoot." His form filled the doorway, joined by the shorter silhouette of Dirlewanger. Both held weapons at the ready, but found no targets.

Keeping the tile open, just a fraction of an inch, Vesely watched the two men as they searched for their prey. The man with Dirlewanger was tall and muscular, dressed in dirty khakis—the kind worn by real archeologists in Egypt. Yet, he carried himself like a soldier, rigid and straight. Vesely couldn't make out the man's shadowed face, but he could clearly see the close-shaven blond hair atop his head, glowing in the twin halogen lamps' stark illumination.

"I have been with this woman—this filth—for five months, Herr Dirlewanger," the man said. "And she escapes you with the help of a single American Cowboy."

"Czech," Dirlewanger corrected, and when the much bigger man looked down at him, he added, "He is a Czech man who fancies himself an American Cowboy. A man prone to flights of fancy."

Vesely nearly aimed his weapon through the crack and showed Dirlewanger a real flight of fancy, but he held his fire. Even with the doctor dead, the Brigade would come for them, perhaps in a less lethal and less organized way, but fifty men were still fifty men.

"Even worse." The man shook his head in aggravation. "And now it would seem that he has filled the shoes meant for me."

What is he talking about? Vesely wondered, but then he quickly realized that the man had been meant to play the hero. He would have swept in, rescued Pasha, become trapped and, just as Vesely was doing now, he would escape through the secret entrance. It was all an elaborate scam.

This told Vesely two things. The long-term subterfuge and planning meant that whatever they were after was truly dangerous, and Pasha was made of strong stuff. Realizing the woman wouldn't be broken, they'd opted for trickery instead, something that brute-force favoring Nazis tended to use as a backup plan when all-out violence didn't get results.

Dirlewanger removed a small flashlight from his pocket, clicked it on and began shining it in the portions of the room concealed by shadow. The beam of light swept toward Vesely, but he didn't dare move. The grinding stone sliding back into place would certainly give them away. Of course, so would being seen.

"Herr Doktor Dirlewanger!" a man shouted from the hallway, the distraction pulling the flashlight beam up, just before it reached Vesely.

"What is it?" Dirlewanger replied in German.

"On the floor!" the unseen man replied. "Gouges. I think the door is here."

Vesely grinned. Pasha wasn't just made of strong stuff. She was also very smart.

Dirlewanger turned and left the room, speaking to the men in the hall. The tall blond man lingered for a moment, squinting into the dark as though trying to intimidate some unseen demon.

"Dieter," the Doctor said. "Come, see."

The man known as Dieter made one last look around the room. For a moment, he stared right at Vesely, but did not seem him in the gloom. Then he was gone, speaking with the men in the ancient hallway.

Vesely lowered the stone slowly back into position, silently resting it back in its original place. When he ducked down into the short tunnel, he was greeted by endless darkness. The only way he knew which way the tunnel led was because the crushing confines allowed him to move in only one direction. Forward.

"Pasha," he whispered, then reached into his pocket for his flashlight. He pushed the button, filling the brownstone tunnel with the bright bluish glow of twenty LED bulbs. The light beat back the feeling of claustro-phobia, revealing more space around him than the darkness had let on. But when he saw Pasha, crouched before him, aiming a gun at his face, the absence of light suddenly didn't seem that bad.

With a sneer, Pasha shook the weapon at his face. "*Who* are you? And if I think you're lying, I'll shoot you."

Vesely listened closely. He'd made similar threats enough times to recognize the truth in her words. She meant it. The problem was, he'd told her the truth the first time. If she wasn't convinced then, why would she be now?

5

"I am Cowboy," Vesely whispered, hands raised as much as he could manage in the tight confines.

Pasha shook the gun at him. "You already said that."

"Please don't shake gun," Vesely leaned away from the weapon and then pointed toward the stone ceiling above him. The block was thick, but not thick enough to completely conceal their conversation if it grew too loud, or if she shot him. "And please keep voice down."

Pasha shook the gun again, this time harder. Vesely grimaced, but understood her frustration. "Dieter was your...friend?"

With no answer forthcoming, Vesely guessed again. "Lover?"

"He said his name was Lawrence Basso. He had real credentials. Published papers."

"Such things can be faked," Vesely said.

"So can accents," she countered. "I trusted him."

"But not enough to show him the entrance?"

"I only discovered it yesterday."

"Did he know this?"

She shook her head, no. "He believed I was lying to him all along. Keeping the secret and the research to myself." She shook her head again, this time in frustration. "If he'd come in alone, I would have shown him."

"Then it's a good thing he didn't come alone," Vesely said, moving away from the entrance.

Pasha raised the gun higher. "My question. Answer it. Now. And no code names."

"My name is Milos 'Wayne' Vesely. I am from Czech Republic. Am gunsli— Am author. Conspiracy theories. About aliens. About Atlantis. About Nazis. Wunderwaffe. Super weapons."

"Book titles?"

"What?"

"Author's can rattle off their book titles without stopping to think about it. What are yours?"

"*Nazi Wunderwaffe and Secret Societies. The Nazi UFO Connection. The Zero-Point Reich. The United States and the Fourth Reich.* My books. If we had Internet, I would show you on Amazon. These are why Survi—Lincoln—contacted me."

"Because you had written about the Nazi conspiracies?" She sounded dubious.

"Actually, because I was on same Nazi hit list as him."

"And you were on the list because of your books?"

Vesely shook his head. "Because I was *right*. I predicted SecondWorld. Saw it coming. Books were meant to be warnings." He slowly lowered his hands. "There is no real way I can prove any of this, but consider the number of dead above? How many Nazis did I kill? Eleven? I suspect you could have been convinced with one or two. And why grenade? You were convinced before then, yes?"

"You want me to trust you because Nazis, who tried to kill almost everyone on the planet just six months ago, got a little overzealous with a charade?"

Vesely frowned. "Good point. How about this? I have not yet killed you."

Before Pasha could react, Vesely shot his hand out, grasped the gun and twisted it out of her hand. As confusion and fear gripped Pasha's face, Vesely repeated the maneuver, placing the gun back in her hand.

She stared down at the weapon in her hand. "But...how do I know you don't need me to guide you through the tunnels below?"

"Are you a good archeologist?" Vesely asked.

"Of course."

"Then you have not seen the tunnels below, either. I suspect you haven't been further than this very spot. Because you're being careful, yes?"

She nodded.

"The time for careful has come to an end."

A second nod.

"Well, careful of ruins. We can be careful for our bodies, which is why I would like to complete this conversation away from—" He pointed up.

"It could be dangerous," Pasha said, looking into the darkness behind her.

"The power source?"

"Yes."

"Booby traps?"

A slow nod. "Maybe."

Vesely failed to contain a smile.

"You're happy about that?"

"Is exciting. Secret tunnels, ancient Egyptian ruins, mystical power sources, evil Nazis, booby traps and a beautiful damsel in distress."

Pasha rolled her eyes. "And a sexist hero."

Vesely smiled. "Sexy?"

"Sex*ist*," she said. "Big difference."

Vesely waved this off. "One last question. *Please* tell me we're looking for the Ark of the Covenant."

"What? No. Why on Earth would you think that?"

"We're in *Tanis*."

Pasha stared at him blankly, not comprehending the significance.

"The Well of Souls—?"

"Is a cave under the Dome of the Rock in Jerusalem."

Vesely sighed and hung his head. "We should go before Nazis kill us."

6

The crawl through the tunnel took twenty minutes, in part because it was as long as a football field, but also because Pasha stopped to inspect every seam, pock mark and deformity for signs of traps, which wasn't easy. Two inches of dirt and dust had collected over the centuries. Vesely knew that if Dirlewanger's men found the entrance to this tunnel, they would take no such precautions.

"Perhaps a faster pace, Dr. Pasha?" he finally suggested, fighting the urge to crawl past her and reveal the absence of traps simply by making it to the end, which was in sight, alive. "It's well known that the Egyptians didn't, in fact, trap their tombs."

Pasha paused. "This *isn't* a tomb."

"Even under the best conditions, any hidden crossbows, trip wires, darts or wooden spikes would have deteriorated by now." He grabbed a handful of dirt and let it fall out between his fingers. "It's all just dust now."

With a sigh, Pasha said, "Perhaps you're right. Archeologists are trained to move slowly. I would have spent a month going through this tunnel with a spoon and a toothbrush."

"Not useful weapons against Nazis."

"I suppose not." She reached out a hand, planting it firmly on the tunnel floor, and then fell forward and through the floor.

Her cry was cut short when Vesely caught her by the belt and held her in place. With his free hand, he angled the flashlight forward and saw a square of the floor was now missing. A moment later, the sound of crashing stone echoed up from some distant chamber.

Hovering over the dark opening, Pasha said, "Back! Pull me back!"

Placing the flashlight on the floor, Vesely took Pasha's belt in both hands and hoisted her back into the tunnel. Safe again, Pasha dusted herself off, cleared her throat and punched Vesely hard in the shoulder. She pointed a finger at his face. "You stick to the UFOs and Nazis. I'm the archeologist."

Vesely looked at the hole. Judging by the time it took the stone to hit the bottom, it was at least fifty feet deep. Had Pasha fallen, she'd have been killed. He nodded. "Agreed."

Pasha moved to the side of the narrow tunnel and lay down on her stomach. Vesely lay beside her and together they slid to the opening's edge. Vesely aimed the flashlight over the side, revealing the space below. The pit walls ended ten feet below, beyond which was open space. Forty feet below that was the floor. The square stone tile that had fallen away rested in three pieces, shattered from an impact with several tall stone spikes.

Pasha turned to him. "Not all traps are constructed from wood. Now, help me across."

The gap was just two and a half feet across, but one mistake could be fatal. With no room to jump, they had to reach over the hole and pull themselves across. Helping each other, they made it over safely, but the trap had added nearly five minutes to their journey.

On the far side, Vesely turned back. "Do you have any fabric?"

"Just the clothes I'm wearing," she replied. "Why?"

Vesely looked her up and down. She was wearing tan cargo pants and an olive drab t-shirt. Fetching in an archeologist kind of way, but not what he was interested in. He frowned. "Turn around."

She squinted at him. "Why?"

"Am taking off pants," he said. "And underwear."

Pasha began to protest, but turned away when Vesely's jeans reached his knees. He quickly stripped off his pants, followed by his boxers. It was a challenge in the tight confines, but he got the jeans back on thirty seconds later. Pasha turned back at the sound of Vesely's knife slicing through the fabric of his boxers. She leaned in closer, chuckling at the pattern.

"UFO underwear?"

"Was gift."

"From Survivor, too?"

Vesely shook his head while using the knife blade to wedge the boxers into the stone crevices on either side of the drop off. "From the girl."

"Arwen," Pasha said, knowing the name. In addition to Lincoln Miller, she'd been the only other survivor out of Miami. Rumor had it, the girl was living with Miller now, but they were being protected by Secret Service and were only seen when they wanted to be.

"She meant as joke," Vesely explained with a shrug. "But I like."

He reached a hand back and Pasha helped him lean back across the opening. With a few pokes of his knife blade, he finished stretching the boxers over the opening.

He gathered dust from the floor and shook it over the draped underwear until the fabric was completed coated.

He sat back. "Not perfect, but if in rush. Maybe we save a bullet?"

A distant explosion shook dust from the ceiling and sent a subtle wave of pressure through the tunnel.

Vesely turned to Pasha. "They will start looking again."

She nodded and started back down the tunnel, still checking for traps, applying pressure on each square tile before putting her full weight on it, but doing so at a faster pace.

When they reached the tunnel's end, they were greeted by a second square opening, descending into darkness.

"Another trap?" Pasha asked.

Vesely shined his light into the vertical tunnel. It descended for twenty feet before ending. There appeared to be a gap at the end, but he couldn't tell how wide, or if there was a tunnel or if it was a dead end. He dug in his pockets for something to drop so he could figure out the distance between the tunnel and the floor, but the grinding of stone on stone from far behind them, locked him in place.

"They've found us," Pasha said.

"Not yet." Vesely swiveled his feet over the hole and threw himself over the edge.

7

Grit exploded around Vesely's body as he shoved his hands and feet against the walls of the hole, slowing his fall. But the walls quickly disappeared, and he fell through open air. The collision with the hard stone floor knocked the wind out of him, but he was otherwise unharmed. He knew his whole body would ache the following day, but for now, the pain was manageable.

Sitting up, he waved the dust away from his head. He took a long breath and felt the powdered stone scratching his throat. He looked up, prepared to shout for Pasha to follow him, but she hadn't waited for his invitation. A plume of dirt wrapped around Pasha's descending form. He rolled to the side just before she arrived, watching as she gracefully absorbed the fall with her knees and turned the energy into a roll.

Still lying on his back, Vesely opened his mouth to compliment her physical abilities, but she lunged at him and slapped her hand over his mouth. With a "shh," she pointed to the ceiling. The square tunnel through which they'd fallen was illuminated from above by a distant flashlight that waved back and forth. Distant voices, shouting in German, reached them a moment later.

Vesely took hold of her wrist and slowly peeled her hand away. "They will be coming."

She nodded and stood, helping him to his feet. As she pulled, he noticed that she was stronger than she looked. And the way she took the fall was impressive.

Vesely scanned the area with his flashlight. They stood in a ten foot square space, empty save for themselves. There was only one exit, a passageway hewn out of solid stone.

"Check the walls," Pasha said.

"For what?" he asked, while playing the light slowly over the flat, tan surfaces. "We should go."

"If there was a sign that said 'acid pool ahead,' you'd want to know about it, right?"

He didn't answer. The walls were featureless.

Vesely made for the exit. "We go now." As he entered the downward sloping tunnel, he asked. "Did Egyptians really use acid?"

"No. I was just making a point."

"Good," he said. "But I also have point. Nazis actually use guns. Is not myth. Very deadly. We go faster now." He flashed a grin that said he was both joking and deadly serious.

"Point taken," she said and motioned him forward.

Vesely was careful to look for anything out of the ordinary, but he didn't slow his pace. If they didn't stay two steps ahead of the Nazis, they wouldn't survive the day. And if this tomb—or whatever it was—didn't have another way out, they'd be equally dead.

The tunnel worked its way back and forth, like subterranean switchbacks, gaining depth, but very little forward distance. After making four turns, the tunnel opened up into a large chamber. Like the room they just exited, it was featureless except for the square of stone spikes stretching up toward the ceiling. Several of the spikes were now broken, a result of the stone tile falling from above. Vesely looked up and saw his boxers, now sagging under the weight of the dirt he'd sprinkled over them.

Then it struck him; he could see the outline of the boxers, but he hadn't shined his light up. The illumination was coming from above. He took Pasha's arm, stopping her in place. The rumble of men rushing over stone pulsed through the air. As suspected, the Dirlewanger Brigade was charging down the secret tunnel with little concern for traps or for their own safety. The man in the lead position regretted his fervor a moment later.

With a shout of surprise, a man dressed as a tourist but clutching a Mini-Uzi, exploded through Vesely's boxers and fell straight down. He landed on the spikes, which quickly impaled him in multiple locations and suspended his body above the floor.

Vesely looked up, meeting the eyes of the man who had been behind the impaled soldier. The second man's shocked expression mirrored Vesely's. Both men snapped out of their shock at the same time. Another Mini-Uzi extended from the tunnel just as Vesely tackled Pasha to the floor, behind the spikes. The stone spires and the dead man's body absorbed most of the rounds, protecting Vesely and Pasha. When the attacker paused to reload, Vesely sat up and fired, striking the stone tunnel's underside.

"You missed!" Pasha exclaimed, having already seen his lethal aim.

Vesely fired again, forcing the man back inside the tunnel, but once again the round struck only the underside of the stone.

"Not miss," Vesely said. "Delay."

"Delay? Shooting stone isn't going to—"

Pasha's words were cut short by a third shot from Vesely's handgun. The round struck stone again, just half an inch from where his first two shots landed. This time, he got the desired result. The old stone cracked down the middle, and the weight of the men atop it did the rest.

Two men screamed, scrabbling for purchase on the stone walls, and then finding none, grabbed at each other. All they managed to do was fall together, striking the hard stone floor fifty feet below. Blood pooled around the pair, who clutched each other in death.

Vesely shined his light up at the tunnel. The gap between the two sides was now too far for someone to cross. Vesely grinned in satisfaction. "They will have to bridge gap or find rope."

Pasha patted his shoulder. "Not too—"

A third German emerged from the tunnel and pulled the pin on a grenade, dropping it into the open space. This time, Vesely wouldn't be able to throw it back. Shoving Pasha ahead of him, he shouted "Go!"

They crossed the thirty feet to the exit in the same amount of time it took the grenade to fall to the floor behind them and explode.

8

Vesely opened his eyes, or at least he thought he did. The view was the same either way—pitch dark. He formed fists with his hands, confirming that he still had a body and wasn't dead. Taking a moment to gather himself, he smelled the dusty tang of ancient ruins mixed with the chemical odor of an exploded hand grenade. He pushed himself up, his body in agony, but the broad pain wasn't nearly as bad as the jolt in his arm. He grunted, placing his left hand over his right triceps. His shirt sleeve was wet and warm. Blood. Even worse, he could feel something hard and jagged protruding from his flesh. A metal fragment, he realized.

"Cowboy?" a voice whispered.

"Am here," he replied.

"I thought you were dead," Pasha said with relief.

"Wounded, but alive. How long was I unconscious?"

"Five minutes. Maybe. One of them shouted taunts at you in German and English, but gave up when you didn't reply."

"Probably for best. Flashlight?" Vesely asked.

"I have it. Shut it off so they couldn't see us."

"You can turn on now. They're gone. Probably think we are dead."

"Are you sure?" Pasha asked.

"They would have shot at our voices. Nazis are impatient."

The light clicked on a moment later, forcing both of them to squint in what felt like blazing sunlight.

"I'm sorry," Pasha said, looking at him with bewilderment in her eyes. "Are you smiling?"

Vesely reached up with his uninjured arm and felt the sides of his mouth. The smile widened. "Would appear so?"

"Why?"

"My name. You called me 'Cowboy.'"

Pasha rolled her eyes. "It's easier to remember than Mako or Mylo or whatever your real name is."

Vesely stood, testing out his muscles and joints. More pain for the following day, but his only real injury was the metal stuck in his arm. He glanced around. They were six feet inside a tunnel leading away from the spiked trap chamber. Safe for the moment, until their enemy found a way down.

Vesely turned his gaze to Pasha. "Cleopatra."

"What?" she asked.

"Your codename."

"That's racist."

"Is not. Is stereotype. Like Cowboy. Simple."

"Having trouble remembering my name, too?"

"No, Dr. Sarah Pasha, I am not." Vesely took the flashlight from Pasha and turned it to point down the brownstone tunnel. "Merely trying to distract myself from fact that we will likely die down here."

"Great. Thanks."

"I will simply call you Pash." When Pasha didn't reply, Vesely added, "Is bad too?"

"That's what my father calls me," Pasha said, her voice quiet.

"Is good, then," Vesely declared in a way that said the decision was irrevocable. He shined the light further down the tunnel, noting that the darkness continued beyond the beam's reach. He turned to Pasha. "Are you squeamish?"

He grinned at her deeply furrowed brow. "Too bad. I need you to pull this out of me." He turned the flashlight on his blood-soaked arm, made more dramatic by the bright white sleeve. He pointed to the metal shard.

"Oh my God!" Pasha hurried to his side, ignoring the blood. "When you said you were injured, I didn't know you meant you were *injured*."

"Is there another kind of injured?"

She shrugged. "I thought you meant you were sore?"

"Am that, too."

Pasha looked over his shoulder. "What's that behind you?"

The reflected light in the tunnel was enough to see by, so Vesely turned to look without moving the flashlight. "I don't—" A sudden and painful pressure on his arm clamped his mouth shut and reopened it a moment later when the pressure transformed into a blazing inferno of pain.

"Hovno!" he shouted.

He spun back around to find Pasha holding a two inch-long shard of metal between her fingers.

With wide eyes, he looked to his arm, which was now missing its metal fragment. He rolled up his sleeve and saw the hole in his arm gushing blood.

Pasha dropped the metal fragment and put her arm over her mouth, stepping away. Vesely was unruffled. He dug into a pocket on the front of his tactical vest. "Are you squeamish or not? Dead men above didn't make you vomit."

"I do better with dead people," Pasha said. "Not so good with flowing blood. If I didn't do it right then, I wouldn't have been able to do it at all."

"Ahh," he said. "Then I thank you, despite rough treatment." He grinned, pulling out a small paper pouch. He tore the top off with his teeth and spit it out. "Another gift from Navy SEALs." Without wiping away any blood, Vesely positioned the packet over the wound and tapped it, sprinkling the powder inside the wound on his arm. With the packet empty, he placed it over the wound and held it in place, applying pressure. He counted to thirty, whispering each number.

"What are you doing?" Pasha finally asked.

Vesely removed the packet, which slid cleanly away. He blew on his arm. The remaining dust flitted away, revealing what looked like a solid scab. "Is a hydrophilic polymer and potassium ferrate."

"A *what*?"

"Dehydrates blood. Forms strong bond." Vesely moved his arm back and forth. It still hurt like hell, but the flow of blood had been completely stemmed and would remain that way until he got to a hospital.

If he got to a hospital.

"Come. We should go."

Before Vesely could leave, Pasha bent down and picked up the discarded halves of Vesely's paper packet and the metal fragment. He raised an eyebrow at her when she pocketed the pieces.

"I can't do anything about bullets and grenades, but this is just littering, and I'm still an archeologist." She shook her head with a grimace. "The damage being done to this site is unforgivable."

Vesely nodded. He was keenly aware that this pristine archeological discovery was being tarnished, not just with grenades and bullets but with the blood and gore that resulted from their use. "I will aim for hearts," he said, hoping to comfort her, but ruined any chance of that by adding, "Brains are messy."

9

"I assume that your return signifies that our adversary is no longer among the living?" Dr. Oskar Dirlewanger said in German to the lone man exiting the secret tunnel they had found just minutes ago.

The man, dressed casually in shorts and a t-shirt with sunglasses dangling from his neck, lifted himself out of the hole, stood and dusted himself off. "Ja, Herr Doktor."

"Very good, Hugo. Was it the explosion?" Dirlewanger asked.

"Ja. A grenade."

Dirlewanger leaned to the side, looking around Hugo. "Karl, Jörg and Steffan are collecting the bodies, I presume?"

Hugo looked down at the floor. "Nein. Dead."

"The Cowboy."

Hugo nodded. "There were traps. The tunnel floor collapsed. It is...impassible."

Dirlewanger sneered.

"Without a rope or planks," Hugo added quickly. "But I believe a rope would be more efficient. We came prepared for such obstacles."

"That we did," Dirlewanger said, turning to Dieter, who leaned against the far wall, arms crossed over his chest. The larger man was no longer dressed like an archeologist. Instead he wore black military garb, body armor and several weapons, including a collection of throwing knives strapped across his chest.

Dirlewanger stepped away casually, but the movement gave Dieter permission to act. He stood up straight and stepped away from the wall, carrying himself like a Doberman attack dog, ready to strike. "You are not one of the Eingefroren, so I will rephrase the Doktor's question, that you might better understand it, and provide a more accurate answer."

Hugo very nervously asked, "Eingefroren?"

Dieter looked to Dirlewanger, a look of shock on his face. "Is he not fluent in German?"

"I am working on it, sir," Hugo said. "I am...*was* French."

Dieter shook his head, exasperated. "Eingefroren means frozen. It is also the word now used to describe the several thousand German officers—" he glanced at Dirlewanger, "—and elite SS soldiers—" he placed a hand over his own chest, "—who were cryogenically frozen at the end of World War II and recently revived. Several hundred of us were killed or captured during the battle in Dulce, New Mexico, many of them by the Cowboy himself. So you see, it is very important to us that there is little doubt about the demise of our skinny Czech friend."

With deliberately slow movements, Dieter drew one of the throwing blades from his chest. "Tell me, Hugo, kamerad...are they dead?"

Hugo's eyes flitted back and forth between Dieter and Dirlewanger, but neither man flinched nor revealed a trace of emotion. "I—I think—"

"*Ehh,*" Dieter grunted in warning.

"I...I don't know." Hugo looked ready to run, but had the terrified eyes of someone who knew that running would be a wasted effort. "It fell close to them. They could not have avoided its blast. But...it was dark. I could not see them. I shouted and taunted in an attempt to elicit a response, but they remained silent. I heard no movement. No breathing."

"Tell me, Hugo," Dieter said. "Are your ears ringing?"

Hugo paused, his eyes going wide. Slowly, he nodded.

"Perhaps you were not hearing so well after the explosion?"

"It is...possible," Hugo admitted. "But it is a fifty foot drop. I could not have inspected their bodies."

"You were right to return," Dieter said. "But you should have spoken the truth."

Hugo looked ready to burst into tears, but he gathered himself, stood straight and snapped his feet together, thrusting his hand up in a Nazi salute. "Ja, Sturmscharführer!"

Dieter responded with a sullen shake of his head. "Were this seventy years ago, and our enemy not so...lethal, I would have already slit your throat."

Hugo's rigid stance didn't falter, but his eyes flicked to the knife in Dieter's hand.

Dieter sheathed the blade. "But you are young and handicapped by your French heritage."

Hugo relaxed, the tension oozing out of him. "Thank you, Sturmscharführer. I will report more accurately in the future."

A knock at the door was answered by Dirlewanger. "Enter."

The door, which hung crooked after being kicked in by Vesely, ground against the floor as it opened. An army of men, dressed like Dieter and armed with an assortment of deadly weapons, stood on the other side, their faces grim. The men, who had previously been dressed similarly to Hugo—as tourists—had donned their battle gear.

"I will change," Hugo said, stepping toward the door.

Dieter took hold of his arm. "You will *not*."

Hugo turned around slowly. "I won't?"

"No," Dieter said, drawing a long flashlight from his belt and turning it on. "*You* will lead the way."

"But—his aim—"

"Is impressive," Dirlewanger said with a grin. "Perhaps you will learn the value of accurate reporting."

"Or how to duck quickly," Dieter added, getting laughs from many of the men dressed for action.

Hugo took the flashlight and turned back to the small hole in the floor. He'd just been handed a death sentence.

10

"Now what?" Vesely said, looking at the wall ahead of them. "Is dead end."

"Is really?" Pasha said.

Vesely turned the flashlight on her. "Now you mock accent? You think I sound stupid?"

"Stupid? No."

Vesely grinned. "I sound exotic, then?"

"More like cute," Pasha explained, "but your comment *was* stupid. The room that gave us access to these tunnels appeared to be a dead end as well."

Vesely pinched his lips to one side. "Good point." He turned his flashlight on the flat walls around them, taking in every inch of their featureless surfaces. "Is unlike Egyptians."

"What is?"

"The lack of decoration. Of hieroglyphs. Of style."

Pasha slowly nodded. "Yeah. There really is nothing here to indicate the tunnel was built by the ancients."

"Except for dust accumulation." He pointed the flashlight to the floor, which would have been clean, or at least cleaner, when it was first created. But a few millennia of dust builds up. In this section of tunnel there was at least three inches of stony grit coating the floor. "Is very old."

"Very old," Pasha agreed.

"And deep."

"All of the ruins in Tanis are buried beneath silt deposited over the area when the Tanitic branch of the Nile shifted, covering the entire area. Over time, it buried everything. Tombs. Homes. Streets. Infrared photos from satellites give us peeks beneath the sands, and some think there could be entire pyramids buried beneath the desert, perhaps even older than those in Giza."

"Would kind of rewrite Egyptian history, yes?"

"That, Cowboy, is why I'm here."

"Under the dirt."

Pasha turned to Vesely. "What?"

He pointed to the tunnel's floor. "Walls are barren, so what we're looking for is under our feet. Under the dirt."

Pasha frowned.

"Something wrong?"

"Just that I should have thought of that."

Vesely shrugged. "Is sometimes hard to think while Nazis are trying to kill you. When I was writing *The Zero-Point Reich*, I became so distracted by first season of Fringe that I wrote very little."

Pasha raised her eyebrow at him. "What's your point?"

"Nazis with guns are worse." Vesely smiled. "Though I sometimes still get distracted by wondering what happened—"

"They all die."

"Hovno! No!"

Pasha laughed, a good hearty one. "Sorry. Sorry. I just wanted to hear you say 'hovno' again. I've never seen the show."

Vesely sighed, but smiled. "A dangerous joke with Nazis pursuing us."

Pasha got down on her knees and began gently sliding her hands back and forth through the dirt. "I didn't realize you were a science-fiction geek. I'll try to be more sensitive next time. If you find something, be careful. It could be the way out—"

"—or it could be trap," Vesely finished, getting down on his hands and knees. "And I am UFO conspiracy theorist. How could I not be a—"

"Found something." Pasha wiped away a patch of dirt at the center of the hallway, revealing a straight line etched in the stone floor. Vesely moved over and helped her clear off more of the line with his hands, but it was full of dirt and it was indistinct.

"Hard to see," Vesely commented as he brushed off the line, which was headed for the far wall.

"Hold on." Pasha dug into her pocket. "They didn't confiscate everything." She pulled a straw from her pocket. "Tool of the trade."

Leaning over the line, Pasha blew through the straw, ejecting the dirt from the line, which was a half inch deep gully, cut into the stone with precision.

"Is clean line," Vesely noted. "As though cut with saw."

Pasha nodded. "The Egyptians were good, but they weren't *this* good."

Working together, they cleared ten feet, revealing a long straight line. Vesely stopped when the line branched in three directions, left, right and straight ahead. He followed it to the right, brushing the collected dust toward the wall. Half way around what looked to be a circle, he coughed. The air, now full of dust, scratched his throat. He unclipped the canteen from his belt, took a small drink and then covered his mouth with the bandanna around his neck. "You want drink?" he asked, holding up the canteen. "Or something to cover mouth?"

Pasha blew a geyser of dust out of the crack and shook her head. "I've been digging in underground tunnels and breathing ancient dust for a good part of my life. I'm used to it."

Vesely clipped the canteen back in place, and returned to work, clearing the other half of the six foot wide circle. "The line does not continue all the way through." He moved to the branch again and cleared away another foot before reaching a second branch, and then another.

With the building excitement that comes from discovery, Vesely set to work, clearing the entire area using his arms. Dust billowed and stung his eyes, but the resolving image made him immune to the irritation.

"It's a symbol," Pasha said.

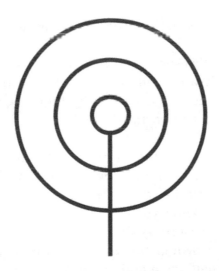

"A large symbol." With the majority of dirt moved into piles against the walls, Vesely leaned down, blowing the dust from the half inch deep lines. He had to pause several times as he grew dizzy, but they soon had the large carving cleaned out.

Pasha stood, looking down at the three rings, cut through by the single line that ended at the beginning of the central circle. "Well, it's definitely not Egyptian. At least, any Egyptian that I know."

"What about non-Egyptian hieroglyphs. Sumerian perhaps?"

Pasha walked around the circumference. "It's too large. There's no reason to make a single character this big."

"Symbols in Nazca are large," Vesely pointed out.

Pasha let out a huff. "Please don't tell me you think the Nazca lines were made for aliens. Or the pyramids for that matter." When Vesely didn't immediately reply, she said, "You do, don't you?"

"Not aliens," Vesely said. "But from the air, from above, yes."

"From above..." Pasha stood on her toes, looking down. "Like a map."

"A map?" Vesely turned his head, looking at the rings. He certainly wasn't an expert in maps, especially ancient maps, but with a flash of clarity, he recognized this one. He gasped. "I know what this is!"

"You do?"

He unclipped his canteen and handed it to Pasha. "Take to line. Pour in. Slowly." When Pasha stood still, looking unsure, he added, "Trust me."

"I barely know you."

"Consider it repayment for saving your life."

Pasha frowned but moved to the beginning of the line. She knelt down and carefully poured the water into the cleanly carved valley. It flowed easily over the smooth surface, sliding toward the rings. At the first ring, the water split, moving forward and encircling the first ring.

Vesely stood at the center of the circles, watching the water expand with a smile on his face. The water reached the second ring and separated again. Then, just after the canteen emptied, the third ring filled as the ten-foot line leading to the rings emptied, thanks to a nearly imperceptible angle in the floor.

With the three rings now shimmering in the glow of his flashlight, Vesely asked, "Now you recognize?"

Pasha looked bewildered as she scanned the circles. "No idea."

"Picture a map," Vesely said. "Three rings of water. Four rings of land. A brass wall around the third ring, a tin wall around the second and a red wall constructed from orichalcum around the central circle." He motioned to the ring around his feet.

Pasha's hands went up to her mouth. "Oh my God."

"Say it," Vesely said. "Or tell me I'm crazy."

"You're not crazy," she said. "It's Atlantis."

Vesely's grin was so wide that not even Nazis could cause it to retreat. "Atlantis."

It was then that the floor beneath his feet gave out and fell away.

11

Hugo leaned out over the tunnel opening expecting his life to end with a thunderous boom. *At least,* he thought, *I won't feel my head explode.* But it didn't. After several seconds of shining his flashlight into the darkness below, he grew confident that the Cowboy was either dead, unconscious or missing.

"Clear," he said, reaching back for the long rope that had been bolted to the stone ceiling.

Dieter handed him the large spool of climber's rope. It was red, thin and flexible—perfect for stopping a fall, but not ideal for climbing down.

Hugo looked down at his bare hands, then up at the soldiers crammed into the tunnel behind him, all dressed for battle. All wearing gloves with non-slip grips.

As though reading Hugo's mind, Dieter said, "You have been given a second chance to prove you are worthy of SecondWorld. Do not cast further doubt on your abilities or your commitment by asking for leniency."

Hugo nodded quickly, recognizing the not so veiled threat. He wasn't accustomed to being pushed around, so the action felt strange and unfamiliar. Before the Fourth Reich reemerged, he'd been the leader of the Milice Suprématie Aryenne or Aryan Supremacy Militia in Paris, France. While they were primarily responsible for graffiti at train stations, in the form of swastikas, and the occasional hate crime against visiting foreigners, as the only white-supremacy group active in Paris, they became important to the SecondWorld movement in Europe. Since those plans fell through, Hugo and his crew found their ability to operate hindered by a Nazi witch hunt and the strident command of their superiors within the now underground Nazi hierarchy. The command included a large number of Old World Nazis, who he had discovered were not nearly as socially adjusted as his pals in Paris.

He shoved the rope over the edge and watched it uncoil fifty feet to the large stone spikes where Karl's impaled body still laid. Hugo swelled with nervousness at the gory sight. His hands began to sweat, and when he took the rope in his hands, it felt like a slippery snake.

I'm going to fall to my death, he thought, but he moved to the pit's edge. Being impaled or killed by the fall would be a merciful death compared to what Dieter would do. The man had the Devil in his eyes.

"Here," Dieter said, handing Hugo a bolt gun. While most rock climbers had to drive a bolt into a stone wall manually, with a hammer or a drill, the design for this pneumatic bolt gun was developed by scientists of the Reich during the long years before SecondWorld had been attempted. It would save them a good twenty minutes. "Secure the bottom away from the trap." He flashed a grin that said he was enjoying every second of Hugo's mental torture.

Without a word, Hugo slowly slid over the side. He instantly felt the tug of gravity and the friction of the rope slipping quickly through his fingers. With a yelp, he dropped ten feet before crushing his fingers tight and arresting his fall. The effort had melted away several layers of skin and amused his commander, who chuckled from above, aiming his flashlight into Hugo's eyes and saying, "Go little spider, go."

With grinding teeth, Hugo loosened his grip slightly and slid toward the floor, each foot peeling away more skin. He nearly plummeted once again when fresh blood from his hand made the rope slick, but his two-foot drop was arrested by Karl's chest.

A mix of relief and revulsion swept through Hugo as he looked down at his feet. He'd survived the climb down, but he now stood atop the impaled body of his comrade, still suspended several feet above the floor.

"Swing little spider, swing!" Dieter called out.

Seeing there was no other choice, Hugo looped the rope around his arm, grasped it as tightly as he could and leapt. If not for the rope wrapped around his arm, Hugo would have simply fallen onto the spikes. As he pushed off Karl's body, most of the force went into pushing Karl's corpse further down, rather than pushing Hugo up. The result was a clumsy, spiraling spin that took Hugo just beyond the stone spikes. He relinquished his grasp and fell to the hard stone floor in a clumsy heap, knocking the air from his lungs.

He coughed and groaned for a moment before his head cleared and he heard Dieter above, hissing his name, prodding him into action. Remembering the bolt gun, Hugo moved to the side wall, placed gun against the wall and pulled the trigger. The gun was loud, but not like a handgun. It drove the bolt two inches into the hard stone, leaving only the metal loop of the hanger. With shaking hands, Hugo tied the end of the rope to an aluminum carabiner and clipped it to the bolt hanger.

Before he could turn his head up and motion that it was safe to proceed, the buzz of gloved hands sliding over rope reached his ears. Dieter descended with such speed and confidence that Hugo had to jump to the side to avoid being knocked over. The buzzing continued as the black-clad Dirlewanger Brigade followed, one by one, quickly fanning out with raised weapons.

"How did you join the Dirlewanger Brigade?" Dieter asked, catching Hugo off guard.

"I—I volunteered."

"Why?"

"The recruitment memo requested men with criminal records."

Dieter looked him up and down. "And you have this? A criminal record?"

Hugo nodded. "I've served time."

"How long?"

"Three months."

Dieter chuckled. "And what is the crime for which you...served time?"

"Destruction of public property."

With a slow shake of his head, Dieter added, "Please tell me that this crime is only the one for which you were convicted. That there are others?"

"Many others," Hugo said, feeling a little defensive.

"Murder?"

Hugo hesitated, and then lied. "Three."

Dieter squinted at him and Hugo hoped the low light would hide any signs of his fabrication. Without revealing what he thought of the confession, Dieter motioned toward the tunnel exit. "They went that way?"

"That's where I last saw them."

Dieter motioned to the doorway. "Lead the way."

Hugo headed for the door, attempting to appear brave and bold, but he noticed the humored looks the other men were casting in his direction. He wasn't sure what was so funny until he realized they were all on high alert, weapons raised and ready to fire, while he, still dressed as a tourist, walked toward a potential ambush, armed only with a flashlight. He unclipped the handgun holstered on his waist and gripped the handle. Pain lanced up his arm when his raw palm hit the hard metal of the grip. He stifled a shout of pain, but was unable to stop the tears building in his eyes.

He managed to raise his weapon, holding it up next to the flashlight, and moved for the tunnel. Keeping his back to Dieter and the men, he entered the tunnel, thankful that the dry air was making short work of the moisture on his face.

The floor, lit by the glow of Hugo's flashlight, revealed evidence of the grenade explosion. Near the tunnel's entrance, the beam of light illuminated a splotch of bright red blood. Hugo knelt by the pool. "He's wounded."

"But alive," Dieter added. "And it's possible the blood is the woman's."

Hugo wanted to argue the point. He knew the woman was in front of the Cowboy when he dropped the grenade, but he kept his mouth shut. Speculation would get him nowhere, except maybe mocked, beaten or killed.

Aiming his flashlight down the tunnel, Hugo said, "This way, then."

"Not quite," Dieter replied, turning back to his men who had just emerged from the tunnel on the far side. He spoke loudly over the continuing buzz of more men arriving. The room now held twenty-five, and the number rose every ten seconds. "What did you find?"

"It leads up," a man replied, "to the above tunnel's intended exit. Nothing more."

Dieter turned back to Hugo, but before he could speak, the sound of a distant, echoed shout emerged from the tunnel.

"The Cowboy," Dieter growled, and then he shouted, "This way!" He charged into the tunnel, shoving Hugo ahead of him.

12

A shout rose from Vesely as his body fell, but he was silenced a moment later when an impact knocked the wind out of him. For a moment, he thought his quick descent had come to an end, but it had really only begun. While he wasn't falling through open air, he continued quickly downward, slipping over a smooth, curved surface like a giant slide. Large chunks of stone—what once was the map of Atlantis—slid all around him, thumping against his body like angry rugby players in the midst of a frenetic scrum.

When a particularly large chunk of curved stone crashed against his wounded arm, he shouted in pain and gave up trying to see where he was going. He had managed to hang onto his flashlight during the fall, but now he used it to illuminate the stones around him. He shoved and kicked while being spun and twisted by the curving tube, until all of the rocky debris was below him.

And then, his ride ended. His feet struck the jumble of stone beneath him, which had come to rest on the floor of yet another tunnel. Feeling thankful that the journey didn't end with yet another fall, Vesely sat up. Before he could scan his surroundings, a yelp spun him around.

Pasha emerged from the steep, curved tunnel, sliding on her back, her feet raised ahead of her. With no time to move out of the way, Vesely took the brunt of Pasha's speedy arrival, her feet connecting hard with his back and sprawling him forward over the field of jagged broken stones.

Vesely grunted as he pushed himself up off of the chunk of rock pushing into his ribs. He rolled over and looked at Pasha, who was focused on their surroundings. "Why did you follow? Could have been dangerous. Could have been trap."

"I heard voices," she said without looking at him. "I think they're coming." Her eyes turned toward the stone debris. "What happened?"

Vesely picked up a fist-sized stone that had once been the inner part of one of the rings. He traced his finger along the curved edge. It came away covered with a goopy substance. "Mortar was water soluble. An Egyptian technology?"

"Not remotely." She touched the viscous material with her finger. "Nothing like this."

"And this?" Vesely asked, aiming the flashlight at the bottom of the slide, which was black, highly polished and reflective. He flicked the wet mortar from his fingertip onto the smooth surface. It quickly slid down, as though repelled from the material.

"Absolutely not. This is something else..."

"High tech," Vesely added, and while Pasha didn't verbally agree, she didn't argue, either.

"But why put this here at all?"

"Is not trap," Vesely said, "But we *are* trapped. It would be impossible to scale back up."

Pasha slid off the slippery surface and stood. "Forward then."

Vesely grunted as he stood, his body already stiffening from the continued abuse. The tunnel was only seven feet tall. Vesely couldn't jump without hitting his head. But it was fifteen feet wide. Though it lacked decoration of any kind, the black floor was constructed from a series of six inch square tiles.

"Oh no," Vesely said with a groan.

"What's wrong?"

"Do you not watch movies or read novels? A tiled floor in ancient ruins full of traps is bad news. Going to be poisoned darts or gas, triggered by pressure-sensitive stones, or the floor will fall away, which is trend for structure's designers."

Pasha leaned down next to the first row of tiles. "You're paranoid."

"I have fallen into two traps already!" Vesely said.

"The tiles are perfectly level," Pasha said.

"Would be."

With a frustrated grunt, Pasha placed her hand on the nearest black square and pushed. Vesely winced, but nothing happened.

"You see? Just a floor." Pasha leaned out, placing her second hand on another tile. Nothing happened.

Nothing obvious, but Vesely's keen eyes caught the slight aberration on Pasha's arms. The fine hair of her forearms stood tall. "Pash!" he shouted, diving forward and tackling her away from the tiles.

A crack ripped through the air, and a buzzing pulse of energy tore through their bodies as they struck the floor. It lasted just a fraction of a second, but it was enough to incapacitate them both for thirty seconds.

Vesely's body and mind both told him to stay down, to rest and sleep and give up, but his will pushed him onward and upward. Sitting up, he shook Pasha. "Alive?"

"Feel like I shouldn't be." Pasha sat up. "What happened?"

"Floor is electrified," Vesely said. "One tile is safe. Two completes circuit. I suspect shock was not immediate because it has been sitting here for thousands of years. Charge took time building up, but now..."

"I don't understand how this is possible," Pasha complained. "It's unlike anything anyone has encountered in Egypt."

"Maybe Egyptians never encountered it, either," Vesely said. "Is high-tech, but maybe not future high-tech. Maybe *past* high-tech."

"An ancient advanced civilization," Pasha sounded confused, but then understood. "Atlantis. Right."

"Or alien," Vesely said.

"Let's stick with Atlantis."

Vesely nodded. "It fits."

"How so?"

"Nazi's believed Atlantis was homeland for Aryan race."

"Because they were supposed to be an advanced race of people," Pasha surmised.

"They viewed Atlanteans as perfect blond-haired, blue-eyed warriors. But not like other ancient soldiers—more polished and disciplined."

"Like the Romans?"

"No," Vesely said. "Like the Nazis. Rigid, cold, calculating and smart. A combination of mental and physical prowess that could be achieved by only true Aryans. Heinrich Himmler, under orders from the Führer himself, created the *Ahnenerbe*—the Ancestral Heritage

Society. Were think tank. They researched great feats of Germanic people, provided evidence for the superiority of Aryan race—creators of sciences and arts. But they also searched for Atlantis. Hoped to recover lost city. Repopulate it. They searched Canary Islands, off coast of Africa because ancient mummies there had blond hair. Believed city was lost because of equatorial freezing."

"So Atlantis didn't sink, it was frozen over? At the *equator*?"

"Stupid, no? Destroyed when ice receded. Himmler sent teams of archeologists and anthropologists around world, to ancient sites, in search of Aryan relics—the remnants of the Atlanteans who fled. They desecrated tombs and destroyed artifacts."

Pasha nodded. "They're destructive past in Egypt is well known." She looked out over the electrified floor. "You don't think this is—"

"—Atlantis? No."

"But the map," Pasha said. "And the technology. This whole...whatever we're in, is buried."

"But the location is wrong. Egypt was well known to Plato. He would have just said Atlantis was in Egypt. If this location is Atlantean, it was not the city itself. Perhaps some kind of outpost. At fringe of empire perhaps. Or perhaps built by those fleeing the original Atlantis."

"Only to be buried again," Pasha said.

"History is full of painful ironies and displaced peoples."

"Huh," Pasha said.

"You have idea?" Vesely asked. "Theory?"

"It's not a very good one, but on the subject of historical irony, what other group of people fled North through Egypt?" She managed a smile. "Imagine the Nazis' surprise if it were the Jews they persecuted who turned out to be the descendants of Atlantis."

Vesely let out a laugh. "Now you are thinking like me!"

Feeling a little less groggy after the brief mental workout, Vesely got to his feet.

Pasha joined him and turned her attention to the electrified tiles. "Now what?"

"We run," Vesely said. "One foot at a time. No stopping. No tripping. I suspect there will not be a delay with the next shock."

Echoed voices reached out of the darkness behind them. The Nazis were closing the distance.

With an urgent whisper, Vesely said, "Go!"

13

Vesely moved as quickly as he could on his tip-toes, which turned out to be quite slow. Keeping his feet inside the eight-inch squares without stepping over the line required careful attention to each step. If his toe slipped over the gap between the tiles, the circuit would be complete, and he'd get a nasty jolt. Even if the shock wasn't enough to kill him, when he fell down and completed multiple circuits, he had little doubt he would be cooked until crispy. The other challenge was that he couldn't step forward slowly. He had to hop so that both feet weren't touching at the same time. This made every step forward precarious at best, and he took short, two-tile steps to ensure his aim remained true.

Pasha followed behind him and seemed to be having an easier time of it, thanks to her smaller feet. "Step on a crack and you're going to get a zap," she sang, mimicking the children's tune.

"I think I prefer breaking mother's back version," Vesely said while balancing on one foot. The distraction threw off his rhythm and he twisted to the side, leaping forward awkwardly. He was forced to jump twice more in rapid succession before regaining his balance. With one foot extended to maintain his equilibrium, Vesely took a moment to control his breathing and wipe the sweat trickling toward his eyes. "No more talk."

Part of Vesely's mind told him he'd be safe no matter what, that his boots would insulate him against the shock, or prevent it from being triggered altogether. But he also knew that the level of protection provided by shoe soles and even vehicle tires had reached mythical status. He knew electricity was content to jump past open space to reach conductive materials, like the human body, which is 70% water. He also had no idea how the tiles really worked. Maybe the skin of his hands completed the circuit, or maybe it was the pressure he applied to the tiles. The later meant an electric charge could be thrown even if he wore twelve inch-tall, rubber, platform shoes.

Starting forward again, Vesely managed to maintain a steady, balanced pace, crossing the hundred-foot long, tiled floor in two minutes. With one last, long-legged leap, Vesely landed on the solid, brownstone floor beyond the tiles and sighed with relief.

The tapping of Pasha's feet turned him around. She was fifteen feet back and approaching calmly, hopping from one tile to the next with grace and confidence. Five feet from the end, a shout rang out from the far side of the space. Pasha turned around instinctively, looking back at the slippery entrance. No one was there, but the pivoting motion spun her sideways. She jumped to the next tile awkwardly, but landed dead center. Her next step was made while falling backwards, and her foot landed in the middle of two tiles.

The crack of electricity was sharp and loud, but brief. Pasha's forward momentum carried her beyond the tile floor. But the powerful jolt had done its job. She fell to the floor in front of Vesely, unmoving.

Vesely dragged her a foot away from the tiles and knelt down beside her. "Pasha!"

He checked her pulse and found nothing. He leaned his face over her mouth while watching for the rise and fall of her chest. He saw no movement and felt no moisture on her lips.

Pasha was dead.

Since derailing the Nazi plans for implementing SecondWorld, Vesely had undergone several trainings with the encouragement of Lincoln Miller. Though he was not part of the U.S. Military, his involvement in saving the world allowed him special access to exercises, training and briefings, sometimes as a student, and occasionally as a teacher, given his extensive knowledge of Nazi activities—both past and present. His official title was Special Advisor to the President on Nazi Affairs, but what it really meant to Vesely was that he would be at the forefront of the battle against modern day Nazism. It also meant that he now knew CPR.

He placed his right hand over Pasha's breastbone and placed the left on top. He raised his body directly over her chest and locked his arms. He shoved down, compressing her chest two inches. He felt a few ribs give way immediately. He cringed at the sound and the pain they would produce if Pasha survived, but with the worst over, Vesely repeated the compression twenty-nine more times, pausing only to deliver two rescue breaths. After repeating this process twice more, it became clear that CPR alone would not work. Were he properly equipped, a portable defibrillator might do the trick, but...

Vesely paused, looking at the electrified tiles that had stolen Pasha's life.

It's my only chance, Vesely thought, and he quickly spun Pasha around, laying her head toward the tiles. He lifted her right arm and laid her hand on one of the tiles. He then unclipped his belt and whipped it out of his jeans. He wrapped the belt around her right arm and held it out over a second tile. Despite leather being an insulator, Vesely cringed as he lowered Pasha's hand toward the tile. He needed to pull her hand away the moment it struck, because a shock that was too strong or too long could make the situation worse.

Can't get much worse than dead, Vesely decided. He dropped Pasha's hand to the tile. The moment her skin struck, he yanked up, fueled by the surprisingly loud crack of electricity.

Pasha's body arced up for a moment, gripped by the jolt's power. Then she fell flat. Vesely lowered his ear over her mouth and watched her chest. "No..." He sat up and started chest compressions again, filled with a deep-seated desperation to not let this woman die.

Fifteen compressions in, her body shook, and Vesely pulled his hands away. "Pasha? Pasha!"

Her eyes fluttered.

Her chest rose, and the action made her wince in pain. Several of her ribs were broken.

When her eyes finally opened, Vesely grinned so wide it hurt. Without thought, he leaned down and kissed her forehead.

"The hell did you do to me?" Pasha asked, and then she let out a small laugh that made her wince.

"CPR," Vesely said, leaning back.

"Broken ribs?" Pasha guessed.

Vesely nodded. "And I had to shock you again."

Pasha pushed herself up, grunting in pain. "That's why I feel numb and tingly all over."

Vesely dismissed the idea with a wave of his hand. "That was from my kiss."

Pasha's laugh became a cry of pain, but she stifled it quickly when Vesely tensed.

Sensing a presence in the room, Vesely stopped moving and started listening. "Hold breath," he said to Pasha, feeling bad about the request since she'd just regained the ability to breathe. But she fell silent.

A gentle scuff and the shaky breathing of a single intruder reached Vesely's ears. He leaned back, drew his revolver and leveled it across the long, black tiled room, aiming his flashlight as well. He could have pulled the trigger and ended the life of the man on the other end, but something made him hold his fire.

He's been watching, Vesely realized. *He could have killed us both, but he didn't.* Vesely lowered his aim a little, keeping the gun ready, but in a less threatening position. Hoping it wasn't a mistake, he waited for the man across the room to do the same.

14

Hugo stood beside a wide circular hole in the floor. He peered over the edge, pointing his flashlight down onto a shiny, curved, downward-sloping surface just a few feet below the floor. "What is it?"

Dieter stood next to him, looking down. "I have no idea."

As more armed men gathered behind them, Dieter's body language stiffened. Hugo sensed the shift in tension would soon be directed toward him, so he attempted to make himself useful. He crouched beside the hole and inspected the smooth edge. It appeared wet. He reached out a finger and dabbed it against the stone. When he pulled it away, a dollop of brown, gelatinous goop came with it. He smelled it and winced.

"What is it?" Dieter asked.

Hugo shrugged and instantly regretted showing any form of indecision. Confusion was weakness and weakness was...well, unacceptable. "It has a strong chemical odor. And it's wet, despite the dry environment. If there was a floor here before, it could have been a trap triggered by moisture."

"Moisture?" Dieter looked unimpressed.

"Perhaps they spilled some water?" Hugo guessed and quickly followed up his continued confusion with, "If they fell inside, it would explain the shout we heard. There is no other exit."

"There is no doubt that they passed through here," Dieter said. "But whether or not this is a trap...that is the question."

"With a rope, we could—"

"Time is short. Sturmbannführer Dirlewanger will catch up shortly. He will want results, not hypotheses."

Hugo leaned out over the edge, trying to see around the curved surface below. "I don't see how we could do it any other way."

"You will," Dieter said before planting his boot against Hugo's back and shoving.

Hugo shouted with surprise as he fell forward. He landed at an odd angle, taking most of the impact on his elbows, which sent stabbing pain up both arms. But the impact didn't slow his descent. Instead, upon hitting the surface, Hugo's speed accelerated. Dieter's mocking laugh pursued him down the spiraling tube, fading with each revolution.

When he reached the bottom, Hugo was on his back, head facing downward. He slammed into the collection of stones that once made up the floor above. The impact turned his vision black for a moment and then filled his eyes with dancing spots of light, like the faeries he believed in as a child.

He nearly shouted out a distant curse when a voice echoed around him, "Pasha!"

Hugo rolled over slowly, blinking his eyes. He found the voice's source more than a hundred feet away, hunched over a prone figure. The Cowboy, instantly recognizable thanks to the Stetson hat he wore. The pair were illuminated by a flashlight that lay on the floor.

Moving slowly and silently, Hugo got to his feet, drew his weapon and waited. He felt unbalanced and didn't want to miss the shot. Better to wait for his head to clear. He could hear Dieter calling to him, his voice distant, but Hugo decided to ignore him. Replying would just alert the Cowboy, whose legendary aim and quick draw would end the confrontation before it began.

Hugo raised his handgun, watching over the weapon's barrel, just in case the Cowboy made a defensive move. But his target was oblivious to everything except the woman lying beneath him. The woman who was apparently dead.

The Cowboy rolled her and performed frantic CPR, his own breathing desperate. Hugo was surprised to find himself fighting the urge to run over and help. Something about seeing this man trying so hard to revive the woman made him want to help. He shook the sensation off and focused on his aim, preparing to fire.

But still, he didn't shoot, deciding he would wait until the woman—the archeologist that both Dieter and Dirlewanger had such interest in—was either revived or left for dead. He nearly fired when the Cowboy gave up on the chest compressions, but then the Czech did something strange.

Why is he turning her around?

Hugo watched as the Cowboy placed one of the woman's hands on the tiled floor of the tunnel and then, using his belt, held the other hand above the floor.

Hugo's gasp at what happened next was drowned out by the crack of electricity. He watched with wide eyes as the Cowboy returned to the chest compressions and a moment later, the woman awoke. Hugo fought the smile that snuck onto his lips, but couldn't deny he was pleased by the Cowboy's inventive and wholly confusing solution.

The floor is electrified.

But the Cowboy still had to die.

Hugo raised his weapon, and without realizing it, brought his flashlight up, too, lighting the Cowboy, who was now leaning over the woman, motionless.

What's he doing? Hugo wondered. *Was he shocked as well?*

Hugo blinked, and in that fraction of a second, the Cowboy drew his weapon and leveled it at Hugo. Stunned by the speed, Hugo froze. And then he wondered why he wasn't dead. And then he realized he hadn't fired, either. Looking over his weapon, he watched the Cowboy tilt the barrel of his revolver toward the floor. A request for peace? A momentary ceasefire? Or a ruse?

The angry voice of Dieter bellowed from the curved tube behind Hugo. "Are you alive? If you are, you better answer me!" The sound made him jump, and the jump made him an easy target, but the Cowboy held his fire.

Feeling grateful for the Cowboy's mercy and angry with Dieter for his lack of it, Hugo raised his hands and let his handgun dangle from his trigger finger. With his head, he motioned for the Cowboy to leave.

He watched as the Cowboy's large hat dipped in a nod. Then the man holstered his weapon, helped the woman up and headed for the exit on the other side of the room. When the pair was concealed by darkness, Hugo called up the tube.

"I'm alive! It's safe!"

A whooshing sound filled the tube, along with a puff of air pressure. Dieter arrived a moment later, reaching the bottom and getting to his feet in one fluid motion, like he'd performed the maneuver every day of his life. He turned on Hugo, fists clenched. "Why did you not respond immediately?"

Hugo turned his head, revealing a trail of blood from where his head had struck the stone. "I reached the bottom with my head facing downward. I struck the stones. I was knocked unconscious."

Dieter paused and looked back at the stones where a stream of men arrived in quick succession, not all as gracefully as Dieter had. He took a long slow breath, which took away some of the menace, but left behind all of his standard vitriol. "I hope you are still feeling up to leading our little adventure." Dieter's hand moved casually to his weapon.

Hugo gave a nod, turned toward the tiled floor and stopped.

"Something wrong?" Dieter asked.

Hugo crouched by the square tiles. He'd seen their lethal ability with his own eyes, but he couldn't say that without revealing he'd let the Cowboy escape. He stood up, fearing Dieter would kick him from behind again.

"We don't have time to wait for Hugo," said Olaf, a soldier whom Hugo knew only vaguely. He was a bull of a man, by far the largest and strongest of them. But he was slow and not exactly bright. Olaf stomped toward the tile floor.

"I'm not sure that's a good idea," Hugo started to say, but it was too late. Olaf planted a single large foot atop the first of the tiles. Nothing happened. But when he brought his second foot down, the floor around him erupted with arcing blue electricity. His body shook, and a warbling scream exploded from his lungs.

A second man—Dolf—shouted, "Olaf!" and jumped forward to help, ignoring Dieter's command to stop. As soon as Dolf's hand latched onto Olaf's arm, the current took hold of both men.

Remembering the Cowboy's tactic, Hugo removed his belt and headed for the shaking men. He looped the band through the buckle, and also ignoring Dieter's order to halt, tossed the belt over Dolf's arm. He pulled hard, cinching the belt tight, and yanking both men away from the floor. The bolts of electricity ceased immediately, despite one of Olaf's feet remaining on the tiled floor.

More men rushed over, checking Olaf and Dolf for signs of life.

"Olaf is dead," one man declared.

"Dolf yet lives," said another.

Dieter stood over the pair, glanced at them both, and then he fired a single shot into Dolf's head. "Not anymore." He then rounded on Hugo and said, "You have five minutes to find a way across or you will join them."

15

Every step Vesely took was punctuated by a stab of pain from one part of his body or another. He could only imagine how horrible Pasha felt, but her tolerance for pain was impressive. She only occasionally let out a grunt. Shock and adrenaline were likely playing a part in her resilience, but he remembered the defiant woman he'd found tied up in the chambers above. She was tough. And strong. Worth more than all the men pursuing them combined.

I will save her, he determined, *or die trying.*

And if you fail? the devil on his shoulder asked.

I will avenge her.

The devil grinned.

Vesely frowned. Through the bouncing glow of his flashlight he could see another dead end up ahead. His anger quickly brewed and vented through his mouth as words. "Every tunnel ends with wall!"

He slowed his approach as they neared the large square surface. He carefully leaned Pasha against the tunnel wall. "You okay?"

She nodded and lifted up the front of her T-shirt, wiping away the sweat from her forehead. She exposed her muscular stomach and dark, lacy bra, but neither site held Vesely's attention. His eyes went right to the center of her chest, where he'd compressed the bones a hundred and five times and broke her ribs. A deep purple bruise was forming. She needed ice. She needed a hospital.

Pasha lowered her shirt and smiled at Vesely's attention. "Now, now, Cowboy, let's wait until the second or third date to get frisky."

Vesely turned red with embarrassment, not because he'd been caught looking, but because he had to let her think he'd been caught looking. If she saw the swelling and purple skin, it could panic her. Despite her strength, if the site of blood bothered her, the pool of it gathering beneath her skin might as well. "Sorry. The eyes wander where they want."

Pasha seemed unruffled and thankfully, didn't tease him. Instead, she looked down at the wet splotch on her shirt. "How deep are we? A hundred feet?"

"Probably more," Vesely said, turning his attention to the floor, kicking dirt to the side, hoping to expose another map etched into its surface.

"Then why is it so warm? Must be nearly eighty degrees down here."

Vesely paused and looked back at her. She was right. Ambient ground temperature below four feet was between 50 and 55 degrees, year round, no matter where in the world you were, even in Antarctica, though Vesely knew from experience that some parts of the frozen south were downright hot and humid. They might be sweating from exertion either way, but they should be shaking from the cold right now. Instead, Vesely was fighting the urge to take off his tactical vest, which was making him hot and itchy.

"Mystery for another time," he said. "Right now, we need to get past this wall."

"What if it's not a wall?" Pasha said.

Vesely raised his hands to the flat surface ahead of them. "How is that not a wall?"

"So far, every obstacle has had a solution."

He couldn't argue with that.

"They're not walls or dead ends, they're gates. With locks and keys."

"Keys?"

She tapped her head. "Our minds. If this structure was built by actual Atlanteans, they might only want people they considered their equals to gain access."

Vesely's eyes widened. "Each wall, each gate, is a test—of *intelligence*."

"Though yours seems to be slipping." Pasha pointed to the wall.

Vesely looked up and gasped. He'd been so focused on the floor that he hadn't carefully inspected the wall. Following the direction of Pasha's pointed finger, he quickly saw a circular aberration. Like the large floor map of Atlantis, there were three rings, but the line that previously connected them was now disjointed and pointing in three different directions. There were also three scooped out depressions on each ring.

"Is test," he said. "Is key."

"Do you know what it is?" Pasha asked.

Vesely raised an eyebrow, communicating that he not only knew what it was, but how to solve it. "Is out of order. Simple."

He placed his finger in the first depression and tried to move the ring. He smiled sheepishly. "Not so simple."

He quickly tried moving the other two rings and neither budged. He shook his head in frustration. "Atlanteans valued order. Rings should be in order."

"What else did they value?"

"Intelligence, of which this is a test. If Nazis are right, they would have valued combat skills, but this is not a battle. What else..." His eyes widened. "Water. The first test required water. Atlantis was surrounded by it. They no doubt depended on it for food. A sophisticated fishing culture. Lovers of the sea."

"You used all of the water on the map," Pasha said with a tinge of worry.

"Not all of it." He wiped his thumb across his damp forehead and it came away dripping. He placed his thumb in the outermost ring's depression and felt the hard stone beneath his finger dissolve. More mortar. As the mortar turned to goo, he pulled down on the ring and it slid smoothly, stopping with the central line facing straight down. He performed the same trick twice more, pausing just before aligning the third ring. "Could be trap."

"I don't think so."

"What if their intention was to kill the more intelligent intruders?"

Pasha patted his shoulder. "Then you should be safe."

He laughed gently and slid the central ring into place. There was a click, but nothing else happened. He pulled his hand away. "Did I do something wrong? Rings are correct. Map of Atlantis is aligned... Perhaps you are right and I am not intelligent enough to solve this puzzle."

"Lucky for you, this kind of thing is my profession." Pasha leaned closer, inspecting the rings. "The alignment of the rings is important, but there is more to it. To open the first gate, you had to add water to the map. It's something that no archeologist in the world would have done. But you recognized it for what it was—Atlantis, and to complete the map required the addition of water."

"We already have done that here," Vesely said.

"So maybe this gate requires further confirmation that we weren't just lucky with the first gate, that we understand that this is an Atlantean doorway. That this isn't just a symbol, but a depiction of Atlantis."

"The gates," Vesely said, the pieces coming together in his mind. "There will be one more after this."

"How do you know that?"

Vesely pointed to the symbol of Atlantis, aiming his finger toward the convergence of the first ring and the straight line. "Atlantis didn't just have three walls, it had three gates, each one able to be closed or opened individually in case of attack from sea, which was unlikely, but they were prepared nonetheless. We have already passed this gate." He raised his finger over the second merger of curved and straight lines. "Which means, we are here. The second gate."

He placed his fingers on the second ring, spacing them evenly, and pushed. The ring slid inward, just a half inch, and then stopped. Without a sound, the wall to the left, which appeared seamless a moment earlier, slid smoothly inward and then to the side.

"You did it!" Pasha said, pushing herself up from the wall. "Not too shabby for a conspiracy theorist."

"I also saved world once," Vesely quipped.

When the door reached a width of four feet, it stopped opening and started closing. "Whoa!" Vesely said and helped Pasha through the door. He had to slide through quickly to avoid being crushed.

The door closed behind them without a sound. Vesely turned and inspected the wall. There was no sign of a door, nor was there a puzzle to open it again. He patted the wall and grinned. "Is good door. Even if they figure it out, only two can enter at a time. Will slow them down."

"That's good," Pasha said, "because... I think..."

Vesely turned around just in time to see Pasha slump against the wall. He caught her before she could fall to the floor. He lowered her down gently and checked for a pulse. She was alive, her pulse strong, but if they didn't start moving again soon, that wouldn't be the case for much longer.

16

"Pasha." Vesely gently slapped her cheek. She'd been unconscious for five minutes. At first he was content to let her wake on her own, but too much time was passing. If they didn't move soon, they'd be making their final stand on this side of the doorway, and that wouldn't last long given the Nazis' penchant for lobbing grenades at him. "Pash, open your eyes. C'mon."

He tried for another minute before giving up. The hallway looked the same as it did on the other side, featureless, long and dark. The third and final gate—if the pattern continued—would be several hundred feet away. But it would also be protected by a trap. A spiky fall protected the first. An electrified floor guarded the second.

So what will protect the third? Vesely shined his flashlight down the hall and found no clues. He felt confident in his ability to make it through, but with Pasha unconscious, things got complicated. He would have never made it past the electrified tiles if he'd been carrying her.

But what choice do I have?

Vesely carefully scooped Pasha up in his arms. She was skinny, but tall and strong. Heavier than she looked. With his flashlight aimed out from under her knees, Vesely started down the hall, one shaky step at a time.

His strength waned after the first hundred feet, and it continued to plummet with each step. The toll of several hard falls and being electrocuted was catching up to him. After two hundred feet, he decided to give his shaking legs a brief respite. He placed Pasha down gently. After releasing her, he remained bent forward for a moment, touching his toes to stretch his tightening limbs. While bent over and close to the floor, he marveled at how black it was. In fact... He aimed the flashlight straight down. Where there should have been a bright ring of light, there was nothing. Just blackness.

It's absorbing the light, he realized. *All of it!*

Vesely's memory kicked in. He recalled reading an article about a super-black material developed by engineers at NASA. It soaked up wavelengths like a sponge, absorbing up to 99% of ultraviolet, infrared and visible light. It was created using hollow carbon nanotubes, something that didn't exist just a few years previous, never mind several thousand years ago. The tiny gaps in between the tubes captured light, preventing a reflection.

But why coat an entire floor with such a substance? Vesely lifted his light. The brown walls were clearly visible.

Vesely lifted his foot, shifting it forward to take a step. But his foot never touched the ground. He stopped, mid-step, looking down at Pasha's hand. Her right arm was extended up over her head, laid across the pitch black floor. While her arm laid flat, her wrist was bent, her hand dangling over open space that looked exactly like the light-absorbing floor.

Whispering a curse, Vesely slowly pulled his foot back. Though he couldn't see it, he knew he was standing at the edge of a precipice. Had he taken two more steps with Pasha, they would have both plummeted to their deaths.

He knelt down and placed his hand on the floor. It was cooler than the air. The microscopic ridges gave the floor a slight grip, like fine sand paper, so he had to reduce the pressure before sliding his hand forward. He found the edge just a foot ahead. It was a perfectly cut, ninety degree angle. After lying on his stomach, he slid up to the drop-off and shined the light over the edge.

Nothing.

The bottom could be ten feet below or a mile. If the surface was covered with the same light absorbing material, there would be no way to see it, even with a floodlight. He moved side to side, hoping to find an invisible pathway—something he could sprinkle dust on and—

Vesely sucked in a quick breath through his nose. The air smelled pure and fresh. He looked around his body and back down the hallway. Where a few inches of dust had collected in the earliest chambers, there was none here...nor was there any in the electrified room. Something about these rooms repelled the grime, or kept the walls and ceiling from deteriorating.

Consumed by exhaustion and frustration, Vesely sighed and lay his head down on the floor. The cool surface felt good on his warm skin. He closed his eyes and quickly felt his body relax. His mind started to fade, lulled toward sleep by a white noise hum.

A revelation exploded into Vesely's thoughts, stopping his descent into sleep. As his consciousness returned, his eyes slowly opened until he looked like a gazing owl.

Vesely lifted his head. The hum stopped. He placed his ear against the floor again. The hum returned.

"My God," he said. Somewhere in the ancient structure, buried for thousands of years, was a machine. And it was *still* running.

Adrenaline, provided by his discovery, fueled the full awakening of his mind. He quickly realized there was one test he had yet to perform on the invisible pitfall. He took a spare magazine for the sound-suppressed SOCOM and popped one of the bullets free. He tossed it out, as far as he could and listened as it struck the far side with a metallic tink, tink, tink. He threw a second bullet, putting less power behind it, and once again, the round struck a solid surface. He repeated his test three more times. The fifth bullet landed just six feet away. He could see it glowing in the light, as though it were hovering, weightless in space.

Aiming carefully with the seventh round, he tossed it gently. It fell toward the invisible floor, just five feet out, and it kept right on going. Vesely quickly lost sight of the round. He listened for it to land, but after thirty seconds, he still heard nothing.

"Nazis?" he said to himself. "Check. Ancient ruins? Check. Bottomless pit? Check. Navy SEALS for back up? Not without cell signal."

At least the bottomless pit is only six feet across, he thought. *And there is plenty of space to jump.*

He looked down at Pasha.

With a woman in my arms.

With no other option and the temptation to lay back down growing, he decided to suck it up and get the job over with. After placing a shiny bullet at the drop-off's edge, he gently lifted Pasha in his arms. His legs jittered from the added weight. He shook out one leg at a time, took five long steps back and focused on the bullet.

Six feet, he told himself. *It's just six feet. If I just fell forward, I could catch the other side. I could jump the distance from a standstill.* He took three deep breaths and then charged forward. As he reached the bullet and leapt, his legs, weary from exertion, reacted clumsily, one smacking the other.

His leap became a tumble.

Forward momentum carried him onward. His arms extended, throwing Pasha to safety on the far side. But Vesely fell short.

Very short.

Only his arms reached the far side, and like his legs, they shook with exhaustion. If not for the rough grip provided by the light-absorbing floor, he would have slipped inside the hole, never to be seen again. As it was, his descent had been delayed—

—only by about ten seconds.

17

"Thirty seconds," Dieter growled, placing the barrel of his gun against the back of Hugo's head.

"Let me think!" Hugo had given up wondering why Dieter was not employing the collective knowledge of all his men and himself. He understood that his grim superior wanted to kill him. Or perhaps just wanted to kill *somebody*, and Hugo was unfortunate enough to be in his crosshairs.

With time almost out, Hugo crouched down. He had just one theory, but to test it required he risk his life. Making the choice to do so was made easier thanks to the gun aimed at his head. His grandfather once told him that remaining stagnant was life's most tempting but most dangerous option. In this case, it would result in his brain being sprayed across the tiled floor in front of him. His grandfather had been right.

He reached out slowly, fingers hovering over one of the black tiles. He noted that the floor was free of dust, decided the detail was insignificant and then pressed his fingers down on the tile. He squeezed his eyes shut and clenched his jaw, but nothing happened.

Ignoring Dieter and the countdown that had nearly expired, Hugo stood and ran to the dead body of Olaf. He dragged the body near the tile floor and stretched out one of the man's hands, repeating the same technique he'd seen the Cowboy employ. He didn't think a shock would resurrect the dead German, but if there was a charge, it would confirm his theory. Using his belt to suspend the big man's arm, he moved Olaf's left hand over the floor.

He quickly positioned the hand over a separate tile from the first. Dieter's countdown had already expired. The only reason the Sturmscharführer hadn't shot him yet was most likely because he wanted to see Hugo's results.

Hugo kept his grip on the belt and lowered the hand. Olaf's body arched up, the dead muscles animated by a massive surge of electricity. Hugo pulled the belt up and Olaf's body slumped back to the floor. He repeated the action, letting the body tense again, removing the hand only after the stink of cooking human flesh reached his nose.

The victorious smile on Hugo's face faded instantly when he turned around to find Dieter's gun leveled between his eyes. "Explain."

"Touching one tile is safe," Hugo said. "Touching two is death."

The subtle twitch of Dieter's finger told Hugo his life was forfeit despite his success, but their conversation was interrupted by a sudden stiffening of the postures in the men around them.

Dirlewanger had arrived. They turned to find him at the base of the slide, being helped to his feet. He dusted himself off and marched up to Dieter. "Report. Why have we been delayed?"

Dieter stood perfectly straight, the line of his chiseled jaw held at a ninety-degree angle. "A deadly trap." He motioned to the bodies of Olaf and Dolf.

"One of them was shot?" Dirlewanger asked. He was not pleased.

"A mercy killing," Dieter said. "He was dying. I sought to ease his pain."

Dirlewanger frowned, but nodded. "And the trap?"

"The tiled floor is electrified." Dieter stepped aside to reveal Hugo. "Hugo has volunteered to test my theory on how the trap is triggered."

Dirlewanger looked Hugo in the eyes, and then looked at Dieter.

Hugo wondered if the Doctor, who was inordinately intelligent, could tell which of Dieter's statements were truth and which were lies. If he could, he didn't care. Hugo wasn't exactly on good terms with the Sturmbannführer, either.

"Proceed," Dirlwanger said.

Dieter turned to Hugo and gave a nod, like he was approving Hugo's decision to brave the electrified floor, but his eyes conveyed a different message entirely: move now or die.

Hugo took a cautious step onto the nearest tile. Goosebumps rose up his leg, causing him to pause. The result of nerves, he decided, not electricity. He looked at the hair standing up on his arms and wished he'd been allowed to put on his black military gear. At least then his fear wouldn't be so apparent.

Standing on one foot, Hugo aimed his flashlight at the next tile on which he intended to stand. Halfway through his step he remembered that both feet couldn't be touching at the same time. He hopped, nearly overshooting the next tile, but he managed to keep his foot within the lines. Forward momentum kept him moving and hopping. Sweat poured over his face, but he ignored it, maintaining a focus unlike at any other time in his life.

After a minute of hopping from one tile to the next, his calves began to ache. A short time later, they cramped, and he feared he would fall. But then the far side of the tile floor came into view and he ignored the growing pain.

Fueled by the end in sight, Hugo took the remaining eight feet in two large leaps. He landed on the far side, planting both feet on the ground. He thrust his hands toward the ceiling. "Yes!"

Remembering he was being watched, Hugo turned around and waved his flashlight back and forth. "It's safe!" His voice echoed across the chamber, bouncing back at him so loud he had to wait for the sound to fade before adding, "One tile at a time. Two will kill you."

As his voice faded again, Hugo was surprised to hear Dieter give the order for all the men to cross. Apparently, having Dirlewanger looking over his shoulder removed any caution the man might normally possess. After a moment of worried glancing, the men began hopping their way across the tiles. Within ten seconds, one of them had stepped on two tiles. An explosion of blue electricity gripped his body and slammed it to the floor, where it writhed and steamed.

The man nearest the victim flinched and fell. He shrieked, knowing his fate would be the same, and then he hit the floor, setting off scores of electrified tiles. The electricity suddenly leaped to the next closest man, who was perfectly balanced on one foot.

Hugo's eyes widened. "Stop! Stay away from one another!"

All but one of the soldiers, including Dieter, froze in their tracks. The one who kept moving was already falling, landing at the foot of another man. The blazing blur of lightning took them both to the floor.

"If you are too close to one another, the floor will see no difference between the feet of two people and the feet of one." He hoped they understood what he was saying.

To his surprise, it was Dirlewanger, still on the far side, who replied. "What would you suggest, Schütze?"

Schütze was Hugo's rank. A rifleman. The lowest possible rank in the SS. But before this moment, he didn't have a rank, so it was actually a promotion. Unfortunately, he didn't really have an answer. So he guessed. "Keep ten tiles between you and the nearest man." He couldn't be sure, but some of the men appeared to be closer than that now, and if the floor was designed with people in mind, the 80 inches between ten tiles should be more than enough space.

The men continued forward, more slowly than before, and evenly spaced, ten tiles apart, minimum. Some kept twenty tiles between themselves and the next man. They also kept a safe distance from the still gyrating and smoldering bodies lying on the floor. As a result, there were no more fatalities. After a minute of watching, Hugo decided to take some initiative and venture forward, heading into the dark tunnel beyond the electrified floor.

18

Vesely's arms shook. His fingers, splayed wide, ached. He tried to swing a leg up twice, but each effort resulted in him slipping a few inches closer to his doom.

"Pasha!" he shouted. "Pasha, wake up!"

Only his echoed shout replied. When it faded, he could hear her breathing softly.

Vesely slowed his breathing and tried to think of a solution. He lacked the strength to simply hoist himself up. If he moved his legs again, he'd likely fall. He moved his feet back and forth, searching for any imperfection in the wall, but it was perfectly flat and smooth. His cowboy boots scraped over the surface, occasionally sticking, but as soon as he tried to push up, his exhausted legs shook from the effort.

This is it, he thought. *Death by an ancient Atlantean trap.* While part of him thought a death at the hands of a lost culture was unique and interesting, it was kind of a silly end for someone who'd saved the world—the entire world. And here he was, killed by a bottomless pit. And the only person available to witness his passing was unconscious and likely to be killed in short order.

Thinking about the fate that awaited Pasha if he fell, Vesely filled his lungs once more and shouted as loud as possible, " Pasha! Wake up!"

This time he was rewarded with a gasp from above.

But the movement created by shouting, along with his perspiring hands, caused him to slip. Vesely's fingers hooked, trying to hold on, but it was no use. The fall was inevitable...until a weight fell atop his hands.

Pasha's head emerged over the side. She reached over the edge and grasped one of Vesely's arms. She was clearly in pain, wincing with every movement, but she spoke with fierce determination. "Swing a leg up!"

Vesely wasted no time kicking a leg up over the ledge. With Pasha keeping him momentarily rooted in place, he managed to get his foot up and over the lip of the pit. Using his leg muscles, his arms and Pasha's help, Vesely pulled himself up. They slid over the edge together in a pile of exhausted limbs and heavy breathing.

They lay on the floor for several minutes, recuperating, until Pasha said, "How is that hat still on your head, and please tell me it isn't clipped to your hair."

Vesely grinned. "Why not?"

"It will totally ruin your manly image."

He shook with light laughter. "Is important for you to think of me as manly?"

Pasha starred at him in silence, a look of peace in her eyes. After nearly a minute of silence, she smiled. "Why couldn't it have been you?"

"Why could what have been me?"

When she didn't answer, Vesely pressed forward. "Pash?"

Her eyes flicked back to his, all of the humor, peace and inner reflection missing. "*Don't* call me that."

"Sorry," Vesely quickly responded. "Is bad codename?"

The silence that followed once more made Vesely squirm, but he resisted the urge to ask her again. 'Pash,' wasn't much of a codename. More of a nickname, really. But something about it bothered her.

"It's what my father called me," she finally explained.

"Is he..." Vesely didn't want to say 'dead,' but she seemed to know where he was going and shook her head.

"He's still very much alive." She pushed herself up with a grunt, leaning against the wall. "He was an archeologist. An American."

Vesely nodded. He knew this already.

"Shortly after 9-11, he left my mother and me. Within a year, he had no contact with us at all. He just disappeared. Until six months ago, just a week after SecondWorld was thwarted. He said recent events had made him rethink his life. His decisions. So I met with him in Cairo. We hit it off. Talked shop. It was like old times. Better than old times. And after just a few days, I was able to forgive him. I told him about this place. About what I thought was here. I'd found an obelisk nearby. It was like a warning sign. Spoke of immense power being buried beneath the sand. Described...something...a device that was as bright as the sun and roared like a lion. Made of silver. Unlike anything else recorded by the ancient Egyptians, and rough. Done in a hurry. Like the object had been found and feared rather than created and revered." Pasha's voice grew quiet. "The shape was..." Her voice trailed off. She shook her head and wiped moisture from her eyes. "The story enthralled my father, and before we went our separate ways, he introduced me to Lawrence."

"Dieter," Vesely said.

She nodded solemnly. "He was charming in an old fashioned way. Rugged. Handsome. And kind. A real knight in shining armor type. Looking back at it now...the timing...the connections. My father used me."

Vesely couldn't hide his surprise. His parents were dead. Had been for years. But they were good parents. Good people. Before their passing he trusted them with every conspiracy theory with no fear of being judged, let alone betrayed. It was unthinkable. "You think he introduced you to Dieter with the *intention* of betraying you?"

"I think he's a Nazi," she said with a sneer.

"Surely, they couldn't have been planning this all along? You don't think he married—"

"I think he left us because of our Arab blood and fell in with white supremacists as a result. If Dieter was only recently revived, there's no way they could have had the long term friendship my father claimed."

Vesely pushed himself up, denying his body further rest. "Then we will not let their deception see fruit." He reached his hand down to her. She took it and let him pull her up. He could see the pain this caused her, but he smiled at the way she fought against it. Pasha was the kind of person Nazis were never able to defeat, even in death. She was brave. Injury, betrayal and looming death couldn't keep her down.

"Your father was a fool," he said.

"That's probably true for any Nazi," she replied.

"More so for your father." He reached his hand out to her. She smiled down at his open palm. "For giving up someone like you."

"My new knight in shining armor." She took his hand.

"Less handsome," Vesely said. "But not a Nazi."

They took two steps before he came to a sudden stop. "Wait!" He quickly picked up the nearest of the bullets he'd thrown over the divide. He leaned down to the black floor and shined his flashlight along the distance. The floor absorbed all the light that struck it, but Vesely's attention was on the bullet. He slid it forward as hard as he could, tracking it with the flashlight. The shiny bullet rolled over the floor, pinging as it spun and bounced, coming to a stop in the distance, against the very normal looking brownstone floor.

"No more holes," Vesely said. He led the way slowly, just in case, keeping his fingers laced around Pasha's and picking up his discarded bullets as they went. They made it out of the tunnel without further incident.

Vesely took a deep breath and let it out with a "phew."

"You're acting like we're out of danger," Pasha said.

"From Atlantean traps," he replied. "I think. The three gates of Atlantis, were likely protected by a garrison of troops, possibly ships. Here, the gates are protected by traps. Eternal guardians. We have survived each one."

"So all that's left is—"

"—the final gate." Vesely looked into the long tunnel ahead. "The final test."

19

Hugo stood in front of the flat stone wall, peering at the strange symbol etched into the surface. He hadn't seen it anywhere else in the ruins or at any time in his life prior. But the Cowboy had. He felt sure of it, mostly because the man had all but vanished, but also because of the three holes in the symbol, each filled with the same slimy mortar.

The symbol meant something...or did something. He was sure of it. But what? And what would happen if he got it wrong? Another trap?

He hated to admit it, but he was beginning to respect the Cowboy. And not just because the man hadn't shot him. He was on the run from a superior force—though even that was debatable since the Cowboy still lived. He and the woman were surviving traps and figuring out puzzles while the Dirlewanger Brigade, although ruthless, were dying quickly. At their current success rate, if the Cowboy was caught, it would simply be because of numbers. As the Cowboy had proven on multiple occasions already, he was the better man.

The better man.

And that was the problem.

Although Dieter and Dirlewanger commanded authority, it was through force and fear, which Hugo had begun to realize were the tools of the unintelligent. Brains always won over brawn in the long run, and the Cowboy seemed to have both.

And honor.

Dieter, his Sturmscharführer, or assault squad leader, would likely kill him before the day was through, simply for giving an inaccurate report, which he did in the first place because the man terrified him. But the Cowboy, Hugo's enemy, had shown him mercy. Granted, Hugo had shown mercy first, by letting the Cowboy care for the woman, but the Stetson hat-wearing enemy had a reputation for being a ruthless killer of Nazis, slaughtering men in their sleep, or in the shower, or with their families.

But Hugo no longer believed that. The Cowboy killed Nazis, but he wasn't a monster.

He wasn't Dieter.

Hugo placed his index finger in the hole in the outermost ring. He pushed down to wipe away a glob of mortar and was surprised when the ring spun. He pushed it further down until it locked in place, the central line pointed straight down. It was only a small mental leap to realize that the other lines should also be pointed straight down. He spun the next two rings until they were aligned, the straight line cutting down vertically through the bottom of the rings.

But nothing happened.

How did he do it? Hugo wondered.

The Cowboy wasn't an archeologist, so maybe it was the woman, Sarah Pasha. She was an expert on ancient Egypt, but although they were in Egypt, he hadn't seen anything to indicate that this was an Egyptian crypt, temple or anything else dreamed up by a Pharaoh. In fact, the electrified floor suggested that there was far more to these ruins than Dirlewanger had let on. As a newer recruit from a country relatively free of Aryan or Neo-Nazi movements, he wasn't trusted with sensitive information. Hugo's organization was small and had operated loosely and independently before being contacted by those carrying out the failed SecondWorld operation. *And now, I'm just a pawn in someone else's game.*

But whose?

He didn't know. With the highest members of the Reich captured or killed in New Mexico, who was in charge? Was it Dirlewanger? Or did he answer to someone else? Hugo didn't like not knowing.

In fact, he didn't like much of anything about his current life.

"Stupid," he said at himself. "So stupid."

With a strong sense of personal defeat, Hugo leaned forward, resting his head on the circular symbol. He didn't aim, but his forehead struck the second ring. He yanked back from the wall, when he felt the symbol move beneath his head.

"Holy Mother of God!" he said when the hidden door slid silently open. "I did it!"

With a broad smile, he stepped through the still opening door and entered the hallway on the far side. His first thought was that Dirlewanger would be proud. But then he realized that Dieter would reach him first and would once again take credit.

Dieter...

Hugo's mood soured.

He felt trapped. His enemy was a good man, but would kill him. His comrades were bad men, but wore the same uniform. He looked down at his vacation getup and realized that, at the moment, that wasn't even true. And he couldn't be sure they wouldn't kill him, either.

I could wait, he thought. *If I don't tell Dieter how to open the door, he won't figure it out. Then I can let Dirlewanger see for himself.*

After successfully crossing the electrified room and telling the others how to follow in his footsteps, he'd already made a small impression. If he got them past the—

A sudden change in pressure turned Hugo around. His flashlight glowed brightly against a solid brown wall. The door, and any sign of it, was gone.

He threw himself at the wall, reaching his fingers out to where he believed he'd find a seam, but it was perfectly smooth. He stepped back, searching the wall with his light, hoping to find a second symbol capable of re-opening the door.

But there was nothing.

My fate is sealed, he thought. Dieter would take his disappearance as desertion, or betrayal, or severe incompetence, any of which would likely inspire the Sturmscharführer to violence.

Only two chances for survival remained.

Find the Cowboy. Beg for mercy. Help him escape.

Or...

Kill the Cowboy himself.

Both possibilities seemed unlikely, but he had no other options.

Hugo turned toward the strangely dark-floored hallway and struck out at a brisk pace. Whatever choice he made, he had to make it before the Dirlewanger Brigade caught up to him. He didn't think Dieter, or the men under him, would make it past the door, but Dirlewanger might. He was intelligent. But the Brigade would likely resort to a problem

solving method with which they were more comfortable—
brute force.

20

"If this final test turns out to be a really long walk," Pasha said, pausing to lean against the tunnel wall. "I'm going to be pissed."

Vesely laughed despite his exhaustion—or perhaps because of it. He leaned forward, hands on knees, to catch his breath. If they were caught anytime soon, the fight would be quick. Vesely feared his quick draw wouldn't be so quick. His arms ached, and he suspected his revolvers would feel fifty pounds heavier. Even if he managed to lift the weapons quickly, take aim and fire, the recoil might pull them from his hands. Firing the big handguns one handed wasn't recommended, but Vesely had built up his forearm strength to compensate, practicing at the firing range until he could fire both weapons at once, like Wild Bill Hickok.

But now, a two-handed traditional firing stance might be required, which would drastically reduce his ability to engage multiple targets—and he would have them, when the Nazis caught up.

He stood up tall again. "I think gate is ahead. Not much further."

"What makes you say that?"

"Hum."

"You want me to hum?"

Vesely grinned. "Listen."

They stood still, holding their breath. In the absolute silence, the hum was easy to hear. Pasha thrust herself away from the wall and turned her head side to side like a wary meerkat. "What *is* that?"

"Sounds like machine. Like engine."

"It's not possible," Pasha said. "Even if the Atlanteans discovered electricity..." She looked at Vesely. "Even if they built an engine... There's no way it could still be running after thousands of years. Even modern man can't build anything that lasts that long."

"I suspect we could," Vesely said. "Is money to be made when things break or decay. And we already know the power is still running. Something electrified floor. But only way to find out is to..." He pointed ahead. The flashlight beam faded into the distance, but he was pretty sure the view didn't end in the pitch black of more open space, but in a wall. Whether it was another dead end or not they would only know when they reached it.

With a sigh, Pasha started forward again. Vesely could see that every step caused her pain. He hurt too, but he could recover on his own. She needed a hospital. She *had* died, after all.

"I'm sorry," he said.

"For what?"

"For...everything." He glanced at her. "Perhaps things would have been better if I did not arrive?"

"You mean, maybe I wouldn't be walking around half-dead and pursued by Nazis?"

"Yes."

"First, a question."

"Anything."

"You have a lot of pockets in that vest. What are the odds that you have some painkillers?"

Vesely gasped, launched into a long-winded string of Czech curses and began searching the pockets. He found what he was looking for a moment later. Two packets of ibuprofen, two of acetaminophen and two of morphine.

"Morphine will make me loopy. Give me the others," Pasha reached out for the packets.

"Will melt your stomach," Vesely protested. "Eat first." He reached into his side pocket and took out a protein bar. "Will be gross without water, but better than stomach cramps."

Pasha took the bar, unwrapped it, took a bite and groaned. "This is supposed to be chocolate?"

"You get used to them."

Pasha took another bite. "Eat them often, do you?"

"Since SecondWorld, have been...mobile. Not much time to eat real food."

"You should slow down," Pasha told him with the kind of tone a mother might use. "Living can't be all about killing."

"There are many Nazis."

"There is also discovery, and beauty, and love, and—"

"Good food?"

Pasha took another bite and couldn't hide her disgusted face. "Hell, yes. But...back to your original question. I am glad you found me. Despite the pain. And the threat of dying...again. I am happy it was you who kicked in that door, and not Dieter." She wrapped the remaining protein bar and pocketed it. She unwrapped the painkiller packets and dry-swallowed all four pills. "In fact, I'm not sure there is anyone else who could have kept me alive all this time, not even your pal, Lincoln Miller."

Vesely chuckled. "Who do you think kept Survivor alive?"

They winced in unison from the laughter.

"No more jokes," Pasha said, still smiling. "They hurt too much."

"But," Vesely said. "Is good for passing time."

He lifted the flashlight from the floor, aiming it straight ahead. The brown wall was now just twenty feet away, and he could now see that the tunnel made a sharp left turn. The hum was louder, too.

"Wait here," Vesely said, drawing one of his handguns. It didn't feel as heavy as he feared, but he was also using his good arm—the one without a ragged hole in it. Pasha lingered back, but never stopped moving toward the turn.

Vesely wasn't expecting there to be Nazis up ahead, but he had no way of knowing exactly what waited around the corner. He led with his weapon, spinning around the corner.

He froze, locked in place, mesmerized by what he saw. The gun slowly lowered.

"What is it?" Pasha asked, picking up her pace.

Vesely didn't reply. He couldn't. Even if Pasha's question could get through to his stunned mind, he lacked the language to adequately describe what he saw.

Pasha was out of breath by the time she reached him, and held it when she stepped around his body and caught sight of the space beyond. Her look of shock morphed into a wide grin. "Now *this* is more like it."

21

What is it? Hugo thought. *A warning? A threat?* There had to be a reason the Cowboy would leave a single bullet standing in the center of the long, invisible-floored tunnel. But what?

Maybe it's just to slow us down as we contemplate the meaning, he thought. He reached out for the round, but stopped short. *Or maybe it is a trap?*

He'd already wasted two minutes wondering about the bullet's purpose. If he stayed much longer, the bullet's purpose wouldn't matter. Dieter would catch up, load the round into his own gun and use it to blow Hugo's brains against the wall.

The bullet bounced off Hugo's finger as he reached for it. He grunted in annoyance, leaning forward to catch it, but then it was gone.

Disappeared.

It fell, he realized. *But where? Into what?*

He searched the area in front of him and saw no change in the light absorbing floor.

"How could it?" he said to himself. Realizing the true danger of this floor, Hugo placed his finger down and slid it slowly forward. Just a foot in front of him, inches away from where the bullet rested, the floor fell away.

"Putain!" He fell back away from the invisible hole, feeling like the floor beneath him could fall away at any second. When he calmed and reminded himself that he made it all this way without falling, he inched back toward the edge. When he found it, he ran his hand along the edge from one wall to another. There was no avoiding the fall, and since he had yet to hear the fallen bullet strike the bottom, he knew the Cowboy had spared his life once again.

But had the Cowboy made it past this obstacle? Or had he fallen to his death?

Hugo dug into his cargo shorts pocket and pulled out a small water bottle. He unscrewed the cap and sloshed the water out, creating a ten foot long stream. He was happy to hear the water strike a solid surface. He put the water away and aimed his flashlight at the floor, slowly moving it up until he saw the glistening water on the far side of the pit, just six feet away. It slowly trickled toward him and slipped over the edge, vanishing into the darkness.

Hugo began to sweat as he slid his feet up to the edge of the pit. Six feet wasn't a small jump, but he didn't dare a running start. As a child in school, he was on the track team. He could jump well from a standstill, but almost always stepped over the line when performing a long jump, a triple jump or anything else that required you to hit a mark before leaping. If he had the same flaw as an adult, he'd fall to his death.

As he bent his knees, he felt thankful for the first time that he wasn't wearing a bulky commando suit. The extra weight and the stiff Kevlar would make this jump tricky.

He lunged forward, shoving with his legs, reaching with his arms. He landed on the far side, slamming against the hard, invisible surface. It knocked the air from his lungs and bruised his elbows, but the real pain came from his shins, which struck the hard, ninety degree corner of the pit.

A hiss of pain came from his lips as he pulled his legs up and inspected his shins. Layers of skin had been peeled away and blood was oozing down both legs. Now, just several seconds after being glad for his lack of military gear, he missed it. The bandages he would have been carrying would have taken care of the wounds. But now, wearing only his faux tourist getup, he'd have to improvise. He took off his outer shirt, a short-sleeve button up with a ridiculous pattern. Using a small pocket knife, his only weapon besides his handgun, he cut the bottom of the shirt into strips and tied them around his legs. Not perfect, but good enough for now.

He looked at what remained of his shirt. There was no way he was putting it on, even if his bright white t-shirt made him an easier target. Plus, it was hot. Really hot. He felt better with it off. He was about to discard the shredded shirt over the edge when he noticed the puddle on the floor.

He stared at it for a moment and then muttered, "Je m'en fou." He leaned down and wiped up the water with the remains of his shirt, erasing all trace of the dangerous trap. When he was done, he leaned up and admired his handiwork. *Maybe Dieter will fall in?*

It would be nice, but he didn't think he'd be that lucky. Dieter, while a savagely cruel man, was also a coward. He would send men ahead of him.

Moving on his hands and knees, Hugo carefully, but quickly crawled up the tunnel, always keeping one hand stretched out ahead in case the floor fell away again. He made good time, and he paused when he reached the brown stone to rest his knees, which had taken a beating on the hard floor.

In the silence, his ears picked up on a strange noise.

A hum!

Something mechanical was running in the underground. But was it coming from ahead or behind? He didn't remember seeing anything that could make such a noise, either in the camp or with the men on the trucks. But that didn't mean—

A gust of wind struck him hard and nearly knocked him over. It was followed by a cacophonous roar. He clamped his hands over his ears and shouted in pain and fright. And then, it was gone.

They're though the hidden door, he realized. *They'll be coming quickly now.*

Hugo climbed to his feet and ran, away from the men to whom he'd sworn allegiance and toward their enemy.

22

Vesely stepped into the large chamber and found himself at the top of a thirty-step stone staircase leading down to a grand doorway. The door and the wall encasing it were metallic, like brushed chrome. The arched door was ornately decorated with a series of swirling designs etched right into the metal. It was framed by three thick bands, each containing a series of symbols that Vesely couldn't read, but which he recognized as a language. The wall to either side was similarly decorated with strings of symbols, evenly spaced, running from floor to ceiling.

Unlike the black, light-absorbing floor, the wall seemed to reflect and magnify light, filling the space with something close to daylight.

Vesely took the first step down. Pasha joined him, placing her hand on his shoulder.

"You recognize symbols now?" he asked, raising up his small digital camera and taking several photos.

"Not a single one." Her hand suddenly gripped his shoulder. "Except that one."

The dread in her voice was an unwelcome sound. "Where?"

She pointed.

He found the symbol at the center of the door, split by the seam running between the two sides. It was ornate, and surrounded by twirling frill, but there was no mistaking the now iconic symbol.

A swastika.

"We shouldn't jump to conclusions," Pasha warned. "This site is ancient. The swastika existed long before the Nazis."

"Represents eternity in Buddhism," Vesely said.

"The Indus Valley Civilization in India used it as early as 2000 BC." Pasha pursed her lips for a moment. "In Hinduism it represents the god Ganesha."

"The elephant!" Vesely said, recognizing the deity.

"Is also symbol for seventh Tirhankara in Jainism," Vesely added, well aware of the Swastika's history. "And is prominent in Armenia, Iran, Ural region, even in Native American tribes, not to mention Celtic, Greco-Roman, Baltic, and of course...Germanic antiquity."

Pasha let out a long sigh. "Right."

"But..." Vesely frowned. "To discount Nazis pursuing us would be foolish."

Pasha took another step downward. "Well, let's see if we can figure it out."

They took the steps together, searching for clues about what they were facing, but short of stumbling on a translation tool, they could only guess. And even if they had a way to translate the text, it would likely take too long.

A tickle on Vesely's neck spun him around. He raised his gun with all the speed he hoped he still had, though it hurt like hell. But there was nothing to shoot. Just a growing breeze.

Vesely squinted into the darkness. The breeze was picking up speed. "Get down!" he shouted, ducking down and pulling Pasha with him. The breeze became an explosion of air, rushing over them. It was followed by the rumble of an explosion that echoed around them.

Vesely stood, waving away the dust kicked up around his head. "Time is running out."

They hurried down the steps, ignoring the symbols around the door and focusing on the door itself. In fact, Vesely's cerebral logic took a backseat for a moment. He took the last step at a near jog, planted his left foot and kicked out with his strong right leg. The door took the kick without the slightest shake, pushing all of the force right back at Vesely, who fell back. He sprawled to the stone floor, flat on his back.

When he looked up, Pasha smiled down at him. "While I appreciate your masculine approach, it seems the Atlanteans were prepared for your Czech thunder."

Vesely couldn't help but return the smile, not just because he liked the sound of 'Czech thunder,' but because Pasha was an amazing woman. It was a rare person who could smile at a time like this. Of course, he probably did look ridiculous kicking a solid wall and falling to the floor.

"Now I understand why you clip that hat to your hair," she teased and turned toward the door, which loomed above them now. She looked up toward the top of the door. "Were Atlanteans tall?"

"Tall?" Vesely asked, then craned his head up to the top of the door: "Ohh...oh my."

"What?"

He shook his head. "Too crazy, even for me."

"Tell me anyway."

"Is book, Book of the Dead. Necronomicon."

"Shop smart," Pasha said. "Shop S-Mart."

Vesely rolled his eyes. "You know this movie reference, but not Well of Souls?"

"Maybe because the Well of Souls is a real place and the Necronomicon is fiction. Lovecraft created it for his stories."

"You might have said something similar about Atlanteans a few hours ago," Vesely countered.

"Tick tock," Pasha said. "Better make it quick."

"Okay. Short version." Vesely collected his thoughts and condensed them. "Some think Atlanteans and Nephilim—you know Nephilim? Biblical giants?" He continued when Pasha nodded. "Necronomicon tells story of ancient demi-gods, drowned in flood. Bible tells story of ancient giants, worshiped by men as gods...drowned in flood. You see?"

Pasha stared at him for a moment. "You're right. That's stupid."

He shrugged. "You made me tell you."

They turned their full attention back to the door. While Pasha examined the symbols around the three-tiered frame, Vesely ran his hands over the ancient metal. It tingled his skin—not because any kind of power ran through it, but because whatever was making the now-loud humming sound, was on the other side.

Pasha traced her finger through an ornately shaped and stylized cross. "Some of these are familiar. They're universal symbols like the swastika. There are crosses, spirals and stars, which are common to several ancient cultures."

"But perhaps began with Atlantis," Vesely said.

"And there is no way to know what they meant to the people who created this door. Just because a symbol was preserved by other cultures, doesn't mean the meaning has been retained. Again, the swastika is the perfect example."

Vesely opened his mouth to reply, but all that came out was, "Ouch!" He yanked his hand away from the door. Blood dripped from his palm.

"What happened?" Pasha asked.

"Was feeling door," Vesely said, searching the surface where he felt the prick. But there was no aberration in the smooth surface, other than the thin etchings. There wasn't any blood, either. "Should be blood."

"What?"

"Where hand was cut..." Vesely leaned away from the door. "Should be blood." Then he saw it, a subtle, but distinctive shape contained within the bending branch of the swastika. He pointed to it. "A handprint. That's where my hand was."

Pasha peered at the smooth print, which was surrounded by similar shapes, like leaves, concealing the hand. "There's nothing there that could have cut you."

"Not now," he said. "Not without hand."

Vesely placed his hand against the print and felt another prick, but this time he didn't pull his hand away. Instead, he pushed.

Nothing happened.

He withdrew his hand, which was now bleeding from a second small hole. "Is final test."

"Like a blood sacrifice?" she asked.

Vesely shook his head. "Worst kind of test. Genetic."

Pasha frowned at this, but then put her hand against the print. She showed no outward sign of being punctured, but Vesely knew she had been when she pushed.

The door didn't budge.

"It seems our heritages don't pass muster," she said.

"Is not surprise," Vesely said. "Like you, I am mutt. Ancestors from all over. The Vesely men like exotic women." He was about to add a second layer to his joke when a voice interrupted.

"Maybe my blood will work?"

Vesely spun around, raising his weapon, only to find his hand caught and a gun leveled between his eyes.

23

"*You*," Vesely said, looking past the gun's muzzle and into the eyes of the man who had spared them earlier. Closer now, Vesely glanced down and looked the man over. His hands were injured, as were his shins. He was also shirtless, looking less like a tourist and more like a vagrant. His trek through the subterranean tunnels hadn't been easy, either.

The man stood there for a moment. Vesely could see he was confused, perhaps trying to make a decision about how to proceed. To simplify things for the man, Vesely slowly lowered his weapon and holstered it. "What is name?"

"Hugo..."

"That is new name, yes? You are not one of the Eingefroren."

The man shook his head, and Vesely wondered if he would realize this interrogation was working backwards. Hugo was the one with the gun. Though the look of fear in his eyes said otherwise.

Perhaps he realizes I could disarm him if I chose to? Vesely wondered. But he didn't think the young man was really a threat—he could have killed them twice already—so he gave the man time to make the right decision on his own. "What is your *real* name?"

"Philippe," he said. "Philippe Augustin, though I never cared for the name."

"You chose Hugo?" Vesely asked.

Hugo nodded. "I was not fond of my parents or their choices."

"Then we call you Hugo. And you are French," Vesely said, stating the obvious. The man's accent was unmistakable. But his features were all Aryan: blond hair and blue eyes. A perfect specimen. "But decent is German? Last name is common in both countries."

"My grandfather moved to France after the War. My father was raised in France. My mother was Norwegian."

"Pure Aryan, then?"

Hugo nodded. "Pretty much."

"Was it grandfather who forged your alignment with..."

"The Nazis?" Hugo guessed. "Not intentionally. He died when I was young. If he spoke about the war, I don't remember it. But I found his trunk when I was older. His uniform. His weapons. And his journal. He...was a good Nazi."

"Not like you," Vesely said.

Hugo's brow furrowed. "What do you mean?"

Vesely raised a single eyebrow as though to ask, *isn't it obvious?*

"You have spared our lives twice. I am Cowboy. Gunslinger. Sworn enemy of Nazis and one of very few responsible for stopping SecondWorld. Killed thousands of Nazis, including many of the highest ranking Eingefroren. You are a bad Nazi."

Hugo's expression didn't change.

Vesely leaned his head to the side, looking at Hugo's weapon. "You haven't even put your finger on the trigger."

Hugo lowered his weapon and smiled. "I'm a horrible Nazi. I only regret it took so long for me to realize it."

"Though you were very nearly a good Nazi." Vesely looked at his wounded arm.

Pasha brought her weapon up, aiming it at Hugo. "That was *him*?"

Vesely gave a nod. "But something has changed him since."

"I told them you were dead," Hugo said.

"And saw how they treat failure when they realized report was false."

"They care about the Aryan race and think nothing of the individual. We are..."

"Expendable?" Vesely guessed.

"Insignificant," Hugo corrected. "When you didn't shoot me, back in the electrified passage, you showed more compassion to me than I have experienced in my life. Some people find God in the trenches, I found clarity. And when I saw the bullet you left behind, once again extending mercy to your enemy, I knew that all of my anger and hatred had been misplaced, skewed by the rambling words of a grandfather I barely knew."

Vesely just nodded, not wanting to admit he had simply forgotten about the bullet he had used to mark the pit's edge.

Hugo looked at Pasha, whose arms were now shaking. "I am not your enemy. Not anymore."

She lowered the gun. "Fine. But if he tries anything—"

"He won't," Vesely said.

"How can you be sure?"

Hugo pointed at Vesely. "Because we all know he could shoot me ten times before I could get off a single shot."

Vesely reached out a hand. "May I see weapon?"

Hugo paused.

"I wish only to inspect, as gun collector."

Hugo offered him the weapon.

Vesely looked it over. "Heckler and Koch P30. A good German gun." He ejected the magazine, turning it around his hand before slapping it back in. "Nine millimeter. Very nice." He spun the gun around and offered it back.

Hugo took it and holstered it.

"I know I'm new to fighting Nazis and saving the world," Pasha said, "But I'm pretty sure you didn't need to give that back to him."

"I suspect he will need it before long," Vesely said to Pasha before turning to Hugo. "How many of the Dirlewanger Brigade are left alive?"

Hugo slowly shook his head. "I'm not sure..." He looked toward the ceiling, whispering out numbers and extending fingers for each. "You killed several. And a good number didn't make it across the electrified floor. At least thirty. Maybe thirty-five."

Vesely grinned.

"Somehow that's a *good* thing?" Pasha sounded incredulous.

Vesely pointed to Hugo's gun, then to hers, and then to each of his three. "Means we have enough bullets."

"More than enough," Hugo said. "They'll probably lose one or two more at the pit." He dug into his pocket and pulled out a single bullet. He handed it to Vesely.

"So," Pasha said. "Now that we're all pals, would you mind trying the door?"

Vesely stepped aside, allowing Hugo to approach the door. He looked at the round and tucked it into his pants pocket.

"Just put my hand here?" Hugo asked while placing his hand inside the palm print. He yanked it back a moment later with an "Oww!" He looked down at the bleeding pricked skin on his palm. "The door is taking skin samples? Why would—"

With a clunk, the doors unlocked, separated with a hiss and opened inward.

"Dammit," Vesely grumbled.

"You realize this is a good thing?" Pasha asked. "Right? Now we're not ducks in a barrel."

"Fish in barrel," Vesely said, frowning deeply. "No, we are not."

"Then what's the problem?"

Vesely looked up, meeting Pasha's eyes. "Means Nazis were right. Aryan race is descended from Atlanteans."

24

"Atlanteans?" Hugo asked. "Like from Atlantis, the mythological city?"

"Is not myth." Vesely motioned to the door. "Is thousands of years old, constructed with amazing skill and can test genetic history of those who would enter through door. You think Egyptians built this place?"

Hugo shrugged. "I'm not an archeologist."

"What are you?" Pasha asked. "Before?"

"I am...nothing really. A thief. A vandal. Can't say I'm a Nazi anymore, can I?" Before anyone could reply, he stepped through the open doors, "What's that?"

Vesely stepped through the gate knowing that its creators would have seen it as a violation. He had Spanish, Gypsy, Asian and even a touch of Native American blood in him. But his thoughts didn't remain on the ancient Atlanteans for long. The brown heap on the floor just beyond the open doors became recognizable as a body, as he stepped closer.

The brown clothing was modern, not ancient. Even if the Atlanteans used modern textile techniques, the style—pants and a collared shirt—wouldn't look twentieth century, nor would the boots. Breaking perhaps every rule of archeology, Hugo reached down and rolled the body onto its back.

Pasha gasped and stepped back. The man wasn't just dead and mummified, he was a Nazi. The pin of an eagle perched atop a swastika on his chest identified him as such. "This is how they knew to follow my work. The Nazis have been here before, they just forgot how to get in."

"Or lost the information at the end of the war," Vesely said.

"But what makes ancient ruins so important?" Hugo asked.

Pasha turned to him, her brow furrowed with confusion. "You don't know why you're here?"

Hugo shook his head. "I wasn't told anything but where to go and who to shoot at. Truth be told, I've never actually shot anyone."

"If you don't count metal fragments in my arm," Vesely pointed out.

Hugo winced. "Right."

Vesely focused on the dead man. The skin of his face was stretched back and dried, revealing his teeth in a grim permanent smile. The husks of his eyes were white and shriveled. And his forehead was caved in flat, and split.

Vesely looked from the forehead to the floor where the body had lain. The stone was stained a darker hue of brown. *From blood*, Vesely thought. "This man fell to his death."

Three sets of eyes and two flashlights turned upward. The featureless and solid ceiling was thirty feet above.

"No trap," Pasha said.

"How did he get high enough?" Hugo added.

"Maybe trap is invisible," Vesely said. "Maybe trap was sealed. No way to know."

Hugo chuckled. "Until someone falls through it. Sorry. Not funny."

A distant shout emerged from the tunnel behind them.

"Speaking of falling," Hugo said. "I think they've discovered the pit."

A second scream followed, sliding quickly away. They listened for more, but only silence followed the desperate cries.

"It won't take them long to find a way across," Hugo said. "We should go."

"First close door." Vesely motioned to the backside of the nearest open door. He escorted Hugo to it, and was happy to see another palm print, this one the reverse of the first. "Left hand."

Hugo's hand hovered over the print. "This hurts, you know."

Angry shouts emerged from the tunnel. Louder than before.

"Quickly!" Vesely shouted and pushed Hugo's hand against the door, only lifting it when he felt Hugo flinch from the prick. The doors quickly and silently slid shut.

Hugo shook his stinging hand. "I would have done it."

Pounding erupted from the other side of the door, making them all flinch.

"Not quickly enough," Vesely said, heading away from the door. The tunnel led upward at a thirty degree angle. The floor was ridged, like there were thousands of tiny stairs leading upward. Fat decorative columns, half buried in the walls, lined either side of the hall. Symbols, some of which actually looked Egyptian, wrapped around each one. Vesely thought Pasha could spend a lifetime just studying the ancient texts and uncovering scores of lost secrets, but she barely glanced at them. She wanted the answer to the same question he did: *what is at the end of the tunnel?*

The hum grew louder, and with each step forward it grew sharper. The tunnel stretched upward for another three hundred feet. Not an easy climb, especially after everything they'd been through, but the end was literally in sight.

Unlike all the other dark tunnels through which they'd traveled, this time they could see the end—not because their flashlight beams could reach it, but because it was lit. Something in the space beyond had power. It was filling the space with light and it was humming.

Not humming, Vesely thought. *Buzzing.*

Like a beehive.

"Hovno!" Vesely picked up the pace despite his instincts telling him to run away, and that fighting thirty assault-weapon wielding Nazis in an open space would be preferable to what he believed they would find.

"What is it?" Pasha struggled to keep up.

Vesely just shook his head and pressed forward, muttering curses beneath his breath. After ten seconds of this, he broke into a jog that immediately burned his leg muscles.

He reached the top just ten steps ahead of Hugo, and what he saw dropped him to his knees. "No..." He turned to Pasha, who was twenty steps back. "Turn around. Go back."

"What? No."

"You have to. We all do."

"Whoa," Hugo said, reaching the top next to Vesely. "Mon Dieu! This is amazing!" He turned to Pasha and dismissed Vesely with a wave of his hand. "Ignore him. You have to see this."

Realizing that Pasha would never turn back into the arms of Nazis without good reason, and without seeing what lay in the gigantic, lit chamber beyond, Vesely stood up, then backtracked and helped her the rest of the way up.

As they walked together, he whispered. "We have to leave."

"Why?"

"Because I would rather be shot than melted."

Pasha's eyes widened. "What?"

"See for yourself." He motioned for the large exit, which was just ten feet away, but the contents of the space beyond was hidden by the steep incline.

Pasha stepped forward slowly, stopping just short of the exit. "Oh my God, is that—"

She knew what it was. They all did. Speculation about the devices' technology, origin, and capabilities had been rampant in the six months since the failed Second-World attempt. That attempt wouldn't have been possible without the device on grand display in the chamber beyond.

"Yes," Vesely stepped up next to Pasha. "Is Bell."

25

The vast chamber stood two hundred feet tall and at least four times as long and wide. The light, Vesely noted, came from the ceiling—the *entire* ceiling. It appeared to be composed of a solid layer of sand, thin enough for the ambient glow of the morning sun to filter through. But it wasn't the only source of light. The bell, which sat atop a hundred foot tall, flat-topped pyramid, cast a shimmering light that shifted around the room's massive, curved walls, giving the appearance of being submerged.

Staircases ran up each side of the pyramid, providing access to the bell, but Vesely couldn't imagine a reason someone would want to get near such a device. When the Nazis experimented with their own bell, clearly inspired by this original, one of the side effects was an energy field that separated elements, including those inside the human body, into their disparate parts. Like oil separating from water, the people would simply slide apart, reduced to slippery globs of elements.

Tearing his eyes away from the bell for a moment, Vesely looked at the rest of the chamber. There were smaller structures—mounds really—that surrounded the pyramid. He wasn't sure if they were decorative or if they served some kind of purpose, but they looked solid. The smooth walls of the giant chamber looked like the inside of a giant egg. And like with an egg, the walls appeared fragile, though he didn't think that was the case, despite the thin ceiling. It had withstood thousands of years of erosion, war and wind. But how?

The bell, of course.

Before the Nile river shifted to cover Tanis with sand and silt, this structure and the bell would have stood out in the open. For what purpose, Vesely could only guess, but he believed the bell was responsible for the creation of this smooth cavern. "Is bubble."

"I thought you said it was the bell?" Hugo asked.

"Is bell, but whole room is bubble."

Pasha saw it a moment later. "You're right. The Nile would have flowed directly over this site, burying what would have been a valley at the time, and filling it in with silt. But not the area around the bell."

"It repulsed earth," Vesely said. "Made bubble."

"And these tunnels must have been carved by Atlanteans who wanted access to the bell after it was buried."

"Or they were trying to get out."

Vesely and Pasha looked at Hugo.

He shrunk a little bit, under their gaze, but added, "You know, if they were trapped inside when the bell was buried."

Vesely thrust a victorious finger in the air. "*Or* if they found site buried upon return."

"Return?" Pasha asked. "From where?"

"Wherever bell took them."

"You mean, like a teleporter?" Pasha asked, even more dubious than usual.

"Or time travel," Vesely said. "Or moving between dimensions."

"What, anti-gravity isn't enough?" Pasha asked, but Vesely barely heard her.

He had nearly forgotten about the Nazis pounding on the door behind them, and the fact that the device that was just four hundred feet away might melt him alive. This was the kind of discovery he'd longed for all his life. He'd been drawn to the unknown and the strange since he was a kid. He investigated ghost sightings in high school. UFOs in college. Ancient mysteries as a young man. And all of the above ever since. His only other passion was the American Wild West and the gunslingers who populated it. And now, here he was, the Cowboy, uncovering an ancient secret that might be the key to some kind of space/time arcane knowledge.

The threats to his life became a distant memory. He took a step forward.

"Vesely," Pasha said, her voice a warning. When he didn't reply, she rephrased. "Cowboy!"

Vesely turned back, hand on his gun. But there was no danger beyond Pasha's stern look.

"I thought you said that thing could melt us?"

The haze clouding Vesely's thoughts cleared a bit. He glanced down and saw that he'd stepped into the chamber. He nodded slowly while his subconscious formed a rebuttal. "I believe it has *potential* to melt people. But, this is original device. Perhaps one of many originals. Nazi bell produced element-separating energy field as side effect from early experiments. Was used as weapon later, but final bells—ones sent to orbit—had no such effect."

"So the Nazis perfected the bell?" Pasha asked.

"Not remotely," Vesely said with a grin. "Anti-gravity might also be side-effect. Nazis who discovered this bell never realized full potential."

"Maybe that's why they want it so badly now?" Hugo said.

Vesely nodded. "Instead of time travel to kill Hitler and prevent war, time travel and give Hitler nuclear bomb. Or travel to dimension where Nazis won war."

"Or maybe it's just a microwave oven," Pasha said. "You need to reign in some of those theories, Cowboy."

"I consider all—"

Pang! A bullet struck the hallway wall just to the right of Pasha. They ducked down, moving down the stairs, deeper into the wide chamber. After dropping out of view, Vesely moved to the side and worked his way back up to the side of the tunnel. He waved at Pasha and Hugo, who had stopped. "Keep going. I will stall them."

"Where are we going?" Pasha asked.

Vesely made a face like he'd suddenly tasted something odd. "To bell, of course!"

"Ohh." Pasha rolled her eyes, and then, dripping with sarcasm, said, "Of *course*. The trans-dimensional, time travel, anti-gravity, people-melting device. It was the obvious choice. Can't believe I didn't think of it."

Vesely smiled. His fondness for Pasha seemed to grow every time she teased him. "If bell is endgame for Nazis, is unlikely they will shoot at us while we are hiding behind it."

"That's actually a good point," she said and then leaned on Hugo. She kept up a brave front, but couldn't hide all of her pain and exhaustion. It was the main reason Vesely wanted her to have a head start. If they all went together, they would never make it down the hundred feet of stairs, across the open two hundred feet to the pyramid and then up another hundred feet to the bell.

Wasting no time, Vesely peeked around the tunnel entrance and caught sight of the enemy, two hundred feet away and climbing steadily. He took aim at the man leading the way and pulled the trigger. The round sliced through the air and the man's skull before the cacophonous report of the firing gun reached the enemy's ears.

The tunnel cleared a moment later as the rest of the men scattered to either side, hiding behind the thick pillars embedded in the walls.

Vesely looked for targets and found none.

"Cowboy," the voice of Dirlewanger called from the distance. "You have managed to impress, as always, but this is one shootout you cannot win."

"How many have you lost, Dirlewanger?" Vesely shouted back. "Twenty men? I have scratch on arm. At this rate, I could have won war for allies by myself!"

Vesely heard the hiss of a command, which he expected, and he leaned out. Two men were hauling up the tunnel, firing their automatic weapons in his direction. He fired once, killing one of the men, but the other was quick and lunged for cover.

Vesely looked back. Pasha and Hugo were near the floor of the giant chamber. They needed just a few more minutes. Sooner or later, Dirlewanger would figure out that ordering an all-out charge was the only way to reach the top. If he did that too soon, Vesely would never make it down to the floor and back up to the top of the pyramid. He had to keep them pinned, and that meant wasting a few rounds. This time, when he heard the hiss of an order, he fired right away, striking only rock, but preventing the next wave of men from advancing.

Keep them talking, Vesely thought. Conversation was the only thing that would really slow Dirlewanger down.

"Sturmbannführer!" Vesely called out.

"Are you ready to surrender Cowboy?" the Nazi Major replied, sounding unjustifiably confident.

"I wanted to tell you about Dulce," Vesely shouted. "I wanted to tell you about how your brave Führer begged for mercy at the end." It wasn't true. Hitler yet lived in the most closely guarded solitary confinement prison in the world, constructed just for him. But very few people knew that. As far as the world knew, Hitler died in Dulce, along with Himmler and most of the rest of the resurrected Nazi hierarchy. "And from what I've seen, he was twice the man that you—"

Screaming orders erupted from the hallway. Vesely rounded the corner, found a target and pulled the trigger. The man dropped, but before he struck the angled floor, five men had taken his place. The Nazis were charging. All of them.

Note to self, Vesely thought, *when stalling a Nazi, do not insult Hitler.*

He rose up, lifting both revolvers, as bullets flew past him. He began pulling triggers, unleashing a flurry of high caliber rounds that Lincoln Miller had dubbed "Cowboy's Righteous Fury."

The trouble was, the Nazis had more men, more guns and more bullets. This was one fight that even the Cowboy could not hope to win.

26

"You don't have to do it," Pasha said between grunts. She and Hugo had made their way down the steps leading to the floor of the massive cavern. She'd nearly fallen twice when Hugo's shoulder bumped her ribs, setting off a cascade of pain that ricocheted through her body like a trapped bullet. But Hugo held her up and kept her moving, actions that Pasha believed were in stark contrast to Hugo's true intentions.

"Do what?" Hugo asked, but she sensed he understood perfectly.

"They have their hooks in you," Pasha said. "Deep. You can feel the tug on your body. On your mind. It's nothing more than a cult, Hugo. Your mind is not your own."

"Shut-up," Hugo's hissed words were sharp and angry, but he never stopped moving.

Gunshots rang out behind them as they reached the flat floor and started toward the bell-capped pyramid. Pasha didn't look forward to scaling those steps. She knew it would hurt like hell. But there was no other option. And she couldn't do it without Hugo's help, which meant she couldn't acquiesce to his request for silence. "You need to think about this."

"What's there to think about?" Hugo continued forward, but his pace slowed. "You and the Cowboy are going to die. That's without question, no matter how good he is. Even King Leonidas died."

"How do you know about Leonidas?" she asked, a bit surprised that the former punk from Paris would know any history.

"From 300."

"What?"

"It's a movie."

Pasha groaned. "Do all men reference movies when talking about history? You know what, never mind. Yes, Leonidas died. But he was the hero. He's the one people look up to. He was brave. He died for his people. He inspired his people. Now look back at Cowboy. He's just one man. Milos Vesely."

Hugo slowed a little more and glanced back at the Cowboy. Vesely leaned out into the tunnel and fired two shots while a hail of bullets cut through the air around him. Shouts of pain emerged from the tunnel in the sudden ceasefire after Vesely ducked back.

"*There* is your Leonidas, alive and fighting—" Pasha stopped and made sure Hugo was looking in her eyes, "—for *you*. He has just met both of us."

"You don't know him?" Hugo seemed surprised.

"I met him just before you arrived, when he kicked in the door and set me free. And he's known you—his enemy—for just minutes. And yet..." She looked back at Vesely. The Cowboy looked down at them and shooed them along. "...he would die protecting you. Have you ever met a man like that in your life? Would any of your Nazi friends do the same?"

The look in Hugo's eyes confirmed they would not.

"Sometimes it's not about how long you live that matters, Hugo, but how you die." Pasha started toward the pyramid again, nearly dragging Hugo along with her. "Trust me. Studying how people died is part of my job. Evil men might make it into the history books, but good men...great men...they can change the world. So you need to decide which you want to be in the end. And we both know that your only chance of survival is him. The Cowboy. So what's it going to be?"

In answer, Hugo stopped.

For a moment, Pasha thought he was going to strike her down and shoot Vesely in the back. She suspected that had been his plan. But then he leaned down and scooped her up in his arms. When she smiled up at him, he nodded and then ran.

They quickly reached the pyramid stairs and headed up. The strain on Hugo was evident in his beet-red face. The stairs were steep, but Hugo maintained a quick pace, despite the extra weight. As they neared the top of the pyramid, bringing them level with the tunnel exit and Vesely across the room, the Cowboy's voice rang out, taunting, "I wanted to tell you about how your brave Führer begged for mercy at the end."

"Oh no," Hugo said. He reached the top, just feet away from the loudly humming bell, but he paid it no attention. Instead, he turned toward Vesely. "He better not—"

Vesely shouted again. "And from what I've seen, he was twice the man that you—"

His voice was drowned out by a violent screaming command from the tunnel, which was immediately followed by a chorus of battle cries and bullets.

Hugo helped Pasha to the far side of the bell, where they'd be temporarily sheltered from the hail of bullets.

Although the Nazi forces were currently firing at an upward angle, striking the distant ceiling, when they reached the end of the tunnel, there would be very few places to hide.

They crouched down together and mutually flinched when the report of Vesely's twin handguns responded to the volley of automatic rifle fire.

When Pasha saw a sly grin emerge on Hugo's face, she knew he was on their side now. He was relieved by the knowledge that every cacophonous round fired from Cowboy's guns meant one less attacker would reach the bell chamber.

But then, all at once, the rumble of Cowboy's thunder came to an abrupt end.

27

Both revolvers ran out of ammo at the same time, leaving Vesely momentarily defenseless against the horde of soldiers charging up the inclined tunnel. Though he had slain several men, the rest continued on, undaunted. They simply leapt their fallen comrades and continued the mad charge, perhaps not fearing death, or perhaps knowing that his handguns didn't hold enough ammunition to slay them all. It was a numbers game, and the advantage was theirs.

Vesely ducked to the side and considered reloading his weapons, but decided against it. They would reach him in the same amount of time, and at close range, he wouldn't be able to compete with their automatic weapons, even with his impeccable aim.

Instead, he ran to the side where the long staircase leading down ended at a broad, flat length of smooth stone. It ran all the way to the floor, a hundred feet below. He dove, holstering his guns in mid air while twisting around to land on his back. His momentum propelled him downward, but the fastest of the Nazi force reached the tunnel's exit when he was halfway down the stone slope. As the man searched for a target, Vesely drew the sound-suppressed handgun strapped to his chest and fired a single round.

The man pitched forward and tumbled down the stairs, leaving a trail of crimson splotches every time his ruined head struck. The second man to emerge, alerted to the presence of a shooter by the gore splashed on his face, ducked back in time to avoid a similar fate.

Vesely reached the cavern floor a moment later, striking hard and rolling several feet before coming to a stop. Bullets tore past his body, chewing a line into the stone floor. He nearly fired a few shots over his shoulder, but thought better of it. The gentle cough off his sound-suppressed weapon wouldn't make anyone duck for cover, and even *he* had to look at a target to hit it.

So he ran, as fast as he could push his aching body— but not for the front of the pyramid. He wouldn't make it up the steps without being cut down. He glanced up as he ran, happily noting that Pasha and Hugo were out of sight.

He reached the side of the pyramid and was just a few steps from being out of view when a spark of pain in his left thigh became a quickly spreading inferno. He knew he'd been shot, but he didn't slow. Didn't care. Pain was manageable. Death was not.

The warm trail of blood running down his leg flowed quickly as Vesely reached the backside of the pyramid and took the tall steps two at a time, vaulting toward the top. Shots rang out from above and were quickly responded to by a burst of automatic rifle fire, the bullets pinging off the bell's metal surface. But the return fire was short lived and was replaced by the voice of an angry German man. Dirlewanger, concerned for his prize.

Vesely reached the top, surprising Pasha and Hugo, who shouted at his arrival before seeing it was him.

"Geez," Pasha said. "With all the bullets zipping about, I don't need a heart attack, too."

Vesely looked from Pasha to Hugo, glancing at their weapons. "Who fired?"

Pasha raised her hand. "They were starting down the steps."

"My gun isn't working," Hugo said, clearly frustrated.

Vesely squinted at Hugo, sizing the man up. He wasn't sure if he could trust him. Was he truly reformed or would he turn on them? Could he risk it?

Pasha, perhaps sensing his internal debate, said, "He's with us."

"You are sure?" Vesely asked, aware that Hugo was listening to their debate.

"I'm with you," Hugo insisted. "I swear."

Vesely looked back to Pasha.

She nodded. "I'm sure."

Vesely reached his hand to Hugo. "Gun." Hugo handed it over. "First round is backwards. I switched when I looked at gun." With a quick yank of the slide, Vesely ejected the backwards facing round, caught it, ejected the magazine, reloaded the round and slapped the magazine back in. He turned the gun around and held it out. "Show me."

Hugo looked down at the weapon for just a moment before taking it, standing and firing three quick shots over the top of the five foot tall bell. A shout of pain rang out in reply. Hugo was laughing when he ducked back down. "Oh shit, I shot Dirlewanger!"

Vesely's eyes widened. "Did you kill him?" As much as he wanted Dirlewanger dead, the man was the only thing keeping the savages under his command from tearing the entire chamber apart. If he died, the bell would be torn to pieces along with the rest of them.

Hugo shook his head. "Hit his arm."

Angry shouts of "traitor," followed in a variety of languages.

"Congratulations," Vesely said. "Now I trust you."

"What are we going to do?" Pasha asked.

Vesely opened the cylinder of one of his revolvers, ejected the spent cartridges and used a speed loader to slap in six new rounds. He snapped the cylinder closed again and repeated the action with the second weapon. Reloading both weapons took him just five seconds. He then stood, raising the guns and fired three shots from each, dropping the men already climbing down the long staircase.

A few rounds were fired in response, but Dirlewanger's angry voice cut them short.

Vesely peeked around the side of the bell and saw an army of men, at least twenty-five, aiming their weapons toward him. Dirlewanger stood in the middle of them, no weapon in site, holding onto his wounded arm. He looked angry, but in control.

When Vesely crouched back, Pasha was staring at him. "So?"

Vesely grinned. "We will use advanced technology." He placed his hand on the bell's surface and felt a surge of energy flow through his body. He yanked his hand away in surprise.

"Did you get shocked?" Hugo asked.

"Was like..." Vesely shook his head. He couldn't describe what he felt. Beyond the physical experience of energy flowing through him, without harming him, there was a kind of bond. Like he could sense the bell.

He looked at the large, brushed metal surface of the bell. Where the Nazi version was inscribed with occult and Nazi symbols, this one contained what must have been Atlantean text. But that wasn't all. There were hand prints, like on the door. Two of them. And apparently, they didn't check for the genetic purity of the user.

But how did it work? There were no other controls.

"With mind," Vesely finally said, confusing his allies. "Is mental interface!"

Vesely slapped his hands against the two prints and immediately felt his body melt away. For a moment, he panicked, but then his senses returned. He hadn't physically melted. It was simply a side effect of the connection he now felt with the bell.

He wasn't sure exactly what the bell could do, and he feared giving it a command it could not understand or complete. He might imagine himself going through time only to find himself launched in the vacuum of space. So he started simple and local, envisioning the results and hoping the strange machine would understand.

"Vesely," Pasha said, as the pitch of the bell's hum grew higher. Her voice carried fear and confusion. "What are you doing?"

"Am giving command," he replied. "But I'm not sure it's working."

"I think it might be," Hugo said.

Vesely turned around to find Hugo and Pasha floating in the air behind him. "It worked!" He thrust his hands up in victory, severing his connection with the bell. Pasha and Hugo dropped to the hard surface of the pyramid's top. Pasha cried out in pain, but it suddenly changed to fear. She rolled away from the side of the pyramid, shouting, "Cowboy!"

A large form rose up. Blond hair, blue eyes and a face full of menace. Without thinking, Vesely charged. Something about the sight of Dieter made him see red and forget all about guns on his hips.

But Dieter was thinking clearly, and he had the reflexes and training of one of the most elite SS soldiers to ever live, or live again. He caught Vesely in midair and used his momentum to throw the Czech.

Vesely sailed out over the pyramid, which fell away below him. As he looked down, Vesely knew this was the end. No one could survive this fall onto the solid, jagged steps now far below. So he turned his body around as he fell and drew his weapons.

But he never got a chance to fire.

28

Vesely brought his gun up to fire at Dieter and snapped his arm to a stop, leveling the weapon at Dieter's head. But the energy from the sudden movement flipped him over. And again. And again. He had jumped out of airplanes before and knew what falling felt like. Aside from the sinking feeling in your stomach as your body accelerated toward terminal velocity, there was also wind resistance and a measure of control.

But this head-over-heels spin was unstoppable.

After his third rapid revolution, he realized that he should have hit the floor already.

He should be dead.

But I'm still falling, he thought, and then he caught sight of the floor, still far below. He wasn't falling at all—he was *floating*.

Anti-gravity!

Vesely swung his arms in the opposite direction of his spin and snapped them to a stop once again, supplying an equal force to the one that started his tumble. He stopped spinning, head in the wrong direction, facing the glowing dome of the ceiling.

Swinging his arms slowly forward, Vesely put himself into a casual rotation that brought him upright and provided him a view of the pyramid, now more than a hundred feet away and growing more distant as Vesely sailed further away, unable to stop his flight.

Dieter was above the pyramid grappling with Hugo, who was clearly outmatched, but fighting for his life. Pasha was crouched behind them, her hands reached up and in contact with the bell. She was controlling it.

She saved my life, Vesely realized. *Time to return the favor.*

He took aim at Dieter, but the Nazi was closely entwined with Hugo, and they were moving. Suddenly, the two men parted. Vesely tracked Dieter, his finger on the trigger, but Hugo beat him to the punch. Hugo fired his weapon, and the force of it flung him away from the pyramid, spiraling through the air. Dieter, struck in the chest, flailed back and spun in the opposite direction.

Pasha was safe for the moment, but Dirlewanger's men would reach her quickly, especially if they could—

Too late. The first of the savage Dirlewanger Brigade, who tortured captured women for fun, floated up above the pyramid, aiming down at Pasha. She was so focused on her interface with the bell that she didn't know he was there.

Vesely took aim, but was struck from behind. He thrust a quick elbow back, intending to dislodge his attacker, but he hit solid stone and nearly dropped his gun as his funny bone sent a sharp tingle up his arm and through his finger. He'd reached the far wall.

Ignoring the elbow, Vesely positioned himself against the wall, planting his feet flat against the stone and slowly leaned forward. When he was lined up with the pyramid's top, he lunged forward with all the strength he could muster from his injured legs. He launched away from the wall like a missile, and despite all of the pain and dire circumstances, he smiled. As a boy, he dreamed of flying, like Superman. He fantasized about flying to the rescue, about saving beautiful women. And now, he was getting his chance.

While in transit, Vesely holstered his two handguns. He wanted to retain the element of surprise, and unleashing them too early wouldn't help. He drew the sound-suppressed pistol, aimed it backwards and fired a string of bullets until the last few rounds were spent and his speed doubled. He ejected the spent magazine, letting it float away, then pulled his last remaining magazine from his tactical vest and slid it into the weapon. He did a quick tally of his ammunition. Twelve in the sound suppressed Mark 23, three remaining in each revolver and two speed loaders, each with six rounds. Thirty total.

More than enough.

"Hey," the man floating above Pasha said as he aimed his rifle at her head. "Lift your hands away from the device."

Vesely wasn't sure if the man realized what would happen if Pasha lifted her hands away. He'd fall atop the bell, slide over its smooth surface and maybe roll all the way down the side of the pyramid. A similar fate would await the other men now slowly rising up over the pyramid, all focused on the bell. But as bad as the sudden return of gravity would be for them, it would be worse for Vesely. He'd drop and slam into the side of the pyramid, returned back to the same fate Pasha had helped him avoid.

That's why she's not moving. She's hanging on for me, trusting that I'll save her.

Vesely took aim, not about to let her faith in his abilities be misplaced.

The Nazi's trigger finger twitched.

Vesely held his fire as he closed to within thirty feet. His upward angle would take him between the three men now floating up, but there were many more men waiting for him on the other side of the pyramid. For his plan to work, he'd need speed on his side and that meant waiting until the last possible moment.

One of the men saw him coming, but Vesely was just fifteen feet away and moving fast enough to reach the trio before any of them could aim without flipping themselves over.

"Keep gravity off!" Vesely shouted to Pasha as he passed and opened fire.

The three men above Pasha spun away, trailing streams of blood that hung in the air.

Vesely's smile crept back onto his face as he rocketed over the top of the pyramid like an honest-to-goodness superhero and left his enemies' jaws hanging slack. He fired quickly, aiming one direction and then the opposite direction, to keep himself from entering an uncontrollable tumble. When the twelve rounds of the Mark 23 were spent, seven men lay dead. Vesely's smile disappeared. His aim, in zero gravity while moving at high speed and spinning, wasn't perfect. He'd missed five shots.

He discarded the handgun and drew both revolvers. But before he could pull either trigger, the enemy below opened fire. Fortunately, only the first few rounds were directed toward him. The rest cut trails all around the cavern as the men spun, out of control. Some of the soldiers were cut down by friendly fire. Others launched toward the ceiling. And a few spun in tight circles, like ice skaters performing never-ending scratch spins. Screams of pain and shouts of confusion filled the air, along with the pungent scent of spent rounds.

Vesely fired both guns simultaneously. One round struck a man floating away toward the far wall, adding speed to his horizontal fall. The second round struck a spinner in the chest. Or the back. Vesely couldn't tell. Rings, like those of Saturn, but made of blood, formed around the man's body, slowly moving outward.

Vesely began to spin, and as some of the men recovered and took aim once again, he fired one weapon at a time. He flipped forward. Fired. Spun sideways. Fired again. Flipped backwards. Fired. And fired again. Still moving forward, Vesely was now spinning and firing madly, but he left another four men dead. As dizziness set in, he closed his eyes and reloaded his revolvers using the two remaining speed loaders. Finished, he opened his eyes and caught a glimpse of the rapidly approaching wall.

How fast am I moving? He wondered. *Fifty miles per hour?* However fast he was traveling, he knew it was fast enough to hurt a lot, if not kill him. He yanked his arms in the opposite direction of his spin, slowing himself down and positioning his feet toward the wall, which was just twenty feet away. He thrust his arms downward and pulled both triggers.

The explosive force of the two handguns loaded with .38 Super ammunition counteracted his forward momentum, but it took four more bullets to slow him to a safe speed. He reached the wall and absorbed the impact with his knees. With his legs bent and his body pressed against the wall, Vesely raised his arms and took aim. His last remaining four shots were true. Four men dropped.

Out of ammo, Vesely holstered his weapons and took stock of the enemy. Several men were floating around the open space around the pyramid. Some out of control, some regaining control through quick bursts of gunfire, which endangered them all. Nine remained, including Dieter, who was somewhere far across the chamber, and Dirlewanger, who had held his fire and was now quickly scaling the pyramid, using the zero gravity to his advantage, while being careful to keep his hand holds. If he reached the bell, and knew how to use it, this fight would end quickly.

With a tense jaw, Vesely took aim and fired the one projectile he had left—himself.

29

Keenly aware that he was little more than a human sized skeet disc with no way to alter his trajectory, speed up or slow down, Vesely let his body go limp and put himself into a lazy spin. To the men rebounding around the room, both dizzy and distant, he would appear to be just another free floating corpse. At least he *hoped* that's how he would appear. There was the chance that some of the soldiers, angered by the deaths of so many comrades, might take a potshot at him just to vent their frustrations.

He risked a peek forward, opening one eye, and saw Dirlewanger standing atop the pyramid, holding onto the bell with one hand, to keep himself upright. He was reaching for his pistol with the other.

Vesely longed for a jetpack, or even a few more rounds of ammunition, but there was nothing he could do but float forward and wait. Dirlewanger on the other hand, was rounding the bell. He tripped, and both feet came off the floor, but he maintained his grip on the lower lip of the bell and began pulling himself back down.

With his feet back on the pyramid, Dirlewanger
raised his weapon at Pasha. He either didn't understand
what would happen when she removed her hands, or he
didn't care. But Vesely did, and he'd arrived just in time.
He passed over the top of the bell, missing it by inches
and would have continued past, all the way to the far wall
if he hadn't placed his hand on the brushed metal
surface. His skin squeaked over the smooth metal, but
then stuck. Vesely spun and kicked out hard. His steel-
toed cowboy boot struck the butt of Dirlewanger's pistol
and sent it soaring toward the ceiling.

Dirlewanger, although older and small in stature, was
also quick and ruthless, and he knew how to fight. Before
Vesely could get his feet beneath him, Dirlewanger struck
him three times in the gut, driving the air from his lungs.
Incapacitated, Vesely couldn't stop Dirlewanger from
driving his head into the side of the bell and shoving him
down to the pyramid's top.

"Sturmbannführer!" It was Dieter, closing in like a
bullet, a sick grin on his face.

Dirlewanger lifted Vesely up, holding him in place.

Vesely tried to speak to Pasha, but before he could form
a word, Dirlewanger delivered a quick chop to his throat,
making it even harder to breathe and impossible to speak.

All around the room, the remaining SS soldiers were
righting themselves and shoving off the walls and ceiling,
closing in for the kill.

Dieter arrived with a war-whoop, driving his shoulder
into Vesely's stomach. Dirlewanger began to fall back from
the force of the blow, but Dieter caught him, and Vesely,
and pulled them both back up. "Herr Doktor, I believe it is
time for us to part ways with the Cowboy."

Dieter punched Vesely in the back of the head, pitch-
ing him forward. He then drove both elbows into the

Czech cowboy's back, slamming him to the pyramid floor next to Pasha.

Vesely heard a knife unsheathe above him. He struggled to move, but he found his body unresponsive, even in the freedom provided by zero gravity.

Dirlewanger's hot breath rolled over Vesely's face as he leaned down and spoke. "You have failed, Cowboy. The bell will once again belong to the Aryan race, where it belongs. We have always been the rightful heirs of the technology...and this world."

"World belonged..." Vesely's strained words came out as little more than a whisper, "...to humanity long before Atlanteans arrived."

"Then you know the truth?" Dirlewanger sounded surprised. "You admit that the Aryan race is the superior species?"

The word species kindled an angry fire inside Vesely.

"Tell me, Cowboy, did the door open for you?"

"Why...do you care?"

"I want to know if I'm about to kill a brother. Misguided though you may be, I will ensure your remains are—"

Vesely was seething with anger but still unable to move. Whatever mercy being an Aryan might grant him, Vesely wanted no part in it. "Door did *not* open for me."

"A pity."

Vesely felt the weight upon his back shift, and he knew Dirlewanger was raising the knife for the final blow.

"No!" shouted a voice.

Hugo.

Gunshots rang out. Shouting followed. A struggle. Vesely slowly rolled over and saw Hugo, now weaponless and in the grasp of Dirlewanger, who was bleeding from two bullet wounds. Dieter moved in wielding the knife that had been intended for Vesely.

"I should have done this a long time ago." Dieter pulled his arm back, coiling to strike.

With a gasp of air that sounded more like a roar, Vesely croaked out, "Add gravity!"

Not resume gravity.

Nor return gravity.

But *add* gravity.

When Vesely felt himself grow so heavy that he couldn't move, he knew Pasha had heard and understood. The seven SS soldiers still in the air screamed as they were propelled toward the stone floor by a force equivalent to four times Earth's normal gravity. They struck hard, moving at over a hundred miles per hour.

Dirlewanger, Dieter and Hugo fell to the floor, their struggle with each other ended for the moment while the invisible force held them to the ground.

Pasha moaned, her hands still touching the hand prints on the side of the bell. She was struggling against gravity to keep her hands in place, but what would happen if she removed them? Would everything return to normal, or would the increased gravity remain?

Vesely feared the latter and struggled to reach her. As he slowly dragged himself over the stone, Dieter's voice rose up behind him. "Cowboy!" The shout carried the struggle of a man fighting an impossible force.

Vesely looked back to find Dieter shaking, but sitting up, knife in hand. With impossible strength, the large Nazi held the knife aloft, took aim and flung the blade with all his strength.

The blade sailed from Dieter's hand, spun once and was yanked downward, traveling just inches forward. It plummeted down and impaled Dieter's leg with enough force to drive it through muscle and bone, stopping only once it struck solid stone.

Dieter let out a shriek of pain, arched back and was slammed to the stone floor as though an invisible spirit had struck him with a sledgehammer.

"Pasha..." Vesely struggled to reach her, but even speaking was difficult. "Normal gravity. Return...to...norm—"

Gravity resumed normalcy in an instant, and Vesely felt lighter than ever. Pasha slipped away from the bell and fell back, unconscious. Vesely lunged forward and caught her head, before it struck the stone floor. He eased her down.

A cackling laugh rang out behind him. Vesely spun to find Dirlewanger standing above him, holding Hugo's pistol.

"You continue to impress," Dirlewanger said, shaking his head. "If only you'd been born German."

"I know several Germans who would like nothing more than to put a bullet between your eyes," Vesely replied.

"Traitors," Dirlewanger grumbled. "And like you, they'll eventually leave this world at my hands." He raised the pistol and squeezed the trigger.

Without a word, Hugo leapt up and took the bullet, charging his former commanding officer, taking him off guard with a flurry of furious blows. His fighting style lacked any form of discipline, but street brawling isn't exactly a useless technique. Three of the first ten blows hit hard and drove Dirlewanger down, where Hugo began kicking him. After seven strong kicks, Hugo lost steam and stumbled back, placing a hand over his now blood-soaked side. He fell back and sat next to Vesely. "Trust me now?"

"Still debating," Vesely said with a chuckle that made him wince.

Pasha groaned and pushed herself up. She looked from Vesely to Hugo and then to Dirlewanger's prone form. He was starting to stir, but he wasn't going any-where fast. Dieter was in a similar state, unconscious with a knife in his leg, but still breathing.

"Are we okay?" Pasha asked. "Did we win?"

"Both," Vesely said, and he was about to thank them both when a chunk of sand fell in his lap. He looked down at the clump, which had fallen apart upon contact. He took some of the sand between his fingers. Realizing where it came from, he turned his eyes toward the glowing ceiling, then groaned. Cracks of bright light raced across the ceiling's surface and continued down into the egg-shaped cavern's wall. The whole place was coming apart.

Vesely sighed. "Fuck."

30

The whole place was coming down around them, crumbling as the cracks spread. It wasn't the thin ceiling that concerned Vesely. It was the walls, which rose high above them on either side. They looked poised to spill inward and bury the pyramid like what should have happened, several thousand years ago. There was no way to know when the walls might crumble, but he didn't want to wait around to find out. The trouble was, there was no way out. Even if they had the strength and the time to make it to the tunnel through which they'd entered, it was a one-way passageway. They would be trapped—like the Nazi they discovered, whose death from falling Vesely now understood.

But how had he entered? The Nazis had clearly discovered the site during the war and based their bell experiments on this device. But the entrance Pasha excavated hadn't been uncovered before. Which meant there was another way in...possibly full of booby traps and miles of tunnel. And that was if they were able to find it, and reach it before the walls crumbled, which Vesely felt was unlikely. Still, he scanned the oval chamber, looking for a way out.

"What's happening?" Pasha asked.

"Walls are going to fall."

"I can see that," Pasha said. "Why?"

"Is bell." Vesely's voice was quiet, his answers coming on autopilot as he searched for salvation. "Gravity changes must have disturbed structure. Or when gravity returned to normal, whatever field held walls and ceiling was shut off."

"Can we reverse it?" Hugo asked.

Vesely had considered this, but he wasn't sure what kind of force had held the walls and ceiling in place. He wouldn't know what command to give the bell, or what would happen to them when he did.

A stream of bright sunlight shot down through the ceiling like a laser beam, striking the side of the chamber and highlighting a passageway that had been invisible before. But it was too far away. The hole in the ceiling quickly grew wider. The falling sand from the ceiling acted like a giant hourglass, counting down the seconds to their death.

And that's all they had. Seconds.

Reaching the tunnel would be impossible. They'd never reach the exit.

Vesely lifted his eyes to the deep blue early morning sky and felt the fresh breeze of the outside world on his face. He knew he could alter the gravity, perhaps delay the walls from falling in and simply leap out of the hole.

But there was another problem.

The bell.

It was an unimaginably powerful technology. The present day Nazis had almost wiped out all of humanity using their less refined versions of the device. What would they do with the real thing? But Nazis weren't his only concern. What would the Egyptians do with such a device? There were plenty of extremists in the country that would love to wipe Israel off the map. But such power, even in the hands of people with good intentions, would be corrupted. What would the Americans do with it? What would any other nation on Earth do?

They would turn it into a weapon.

But even if it was simply buried, it would be discovered. The crater left in its wake would draw a lot of attention. And once the bell was uncovered, wars would be fought to claim it.

A sliver of white in the deep blue sky caught Vesely's attention. The moon. It's otherworldly sight reminded Vesely about his new theory for the location of Atlantis, which in turn triggered a cascade of theories about what the bell was truly capable of doing.

"Hands on the bell!" he shouted, as the walls began to fall in.

Pasha and Hugo acted quickly, placing their hands on the surface of the bell, while Vesely placed his hands within the etched palm prints. But they weren't alone. Dieter thumped up against the device, lifting Dirlewanger against it with him. He glared at Vesely, projecting death, but he didn't try to fight. Vesely knew that would change the moment they were all safe...if such a thing was possible, but there was no time to attempt dislodging the pair, as sand rained down around them.

Of course, if this worked, there were other possibilities to consider.

Vesely smiled and made sure that Dieter saw him.

Dirlewanger opened his eyes and saw the smile too. His frown deepened as Vesely's smile grew larger. Dirlewanger began to shout, but his voice was drowned out by the rumble of collapsing walls and the rising hum of the bell.

Vesely closed his eyes and focused on a location.

And a date.

The feeling of sun on his skin disappeared. The air smelled of blood, grit and antiseptic. Voices filled the air, muffled by a doorway.

He slowly opened his eyes.

They were in a room. A hospital room. The bell filled much of the space, filling half of the room and scraping the ceiling.

Despite the menace in Dieter's eyes, he stood back and looked around, stunned by the sudden change in location.

"Where are we?" Dirlewanger asked, pushing himself up. "Where did you bring us?"

"First General Hospital, Paris, France."

"Paris?" Hugo said and dashed to the window. He threw it open to reveal a war torn city. "What the..."

"June 1st," Vesely added. "1945."

"What!" Dirlewanger shouted.

Vesely couldn't hide his grin. "I see you have read own bio."

"Are you sure we should be here?" Pasha asked, holding Vesely's arm. "Couldn't we change the past? Create a paradox or something?"

"We are not changing past. We are completing it." Vesely pointed at Dirlewanger. "History says he is captured here, on this date, in this hospital. Is handed over to Polish. Is beaten. Tortured. Dies from injuries on fifth."

Dirlewanger ducked down, grasped the knife in Dieter's leg and yanked it free. Dieter wailed and fell to the floor. Dirlewanger charged and swung. His aim was true, but he hadn't predicted the sudden, momentary change in gravity.

Dirlewanger tripped as his feet stuck to the floor. He fell past Vesely and struck his head on a bedpost, falling to the side, unconscious once more.

Dieter reclaimed his knife and hopped for the door. If he escaped, he might actually be able to connect with underground German forces still in the city.

Hugo left the window, dashed across the room and dove at Dieter. The pair hit the wooden door and crashed through it, slamming into the hallway. Screams erupted from the hall as patients and nurses fled the scene.

Hugo drove his fist into Dieter's back three times, pounding his former commander. But Dieter wasn't defenseless. He thrust his elbow back and up, connecting with Hugo's chin, knocking him back. Then he took aim with the knife, twisting it up towards Hugo's chest.

Angry French voices rang out. "Lâchez votre arme!"

Hugo responded in perfect French, his native language. "Aider! Il est un Nazi!"

As the knife came up toward Hugo's heart, a shot rang out. Dieter took a round to the side of his head and fell slack like a discarded child's toy. But the shot hadn't come from the police. It had come from the hospital room. Hugo turned to find Vesely grinning, holding his smoking revolver. "Remembered bullet you gave me."

Hugo ducked back into the room as voices yelled at him to stop. He dove forward, reaching for the bell.

Vesely turned to Pasha. Her hands were on the device already. As soon as Hugo's palms struck the bell's surface, the trio disappeared without a sound.

31

Vesely realized his error a second after he felt the hospital room vanish. He had willed the bell to whisk them away, but he hadn't picked a location. Hugo and Pasha were still with him, but appeared to be in some kind of trance, unaware of what was happening. Vesely, on the other hand, could see and feel everything.

Like projected memories, worlds and times shifted around him. He saw just glimpses of each, but when he did, the visual stimuli came with a full understanding of what he saw. Entire worlds, filled with people and their stories. Heroes, villains, wars and monsters.

He saw a man standing atop a tall building, facing off against a 300-foot tall monster whose dark body glowed with patches of orange fury. It was unlike anything Vesely had ever seen or hoped to see again.

Then there was a team of four men and one women. Special Forces, like Survivor, but fighting a creature made of stone, aided by a little girl. Vesely felt a kind of kinship with them, like they, more than anyone he'd ever met, would understand the way he saw the world.

Then there was a boy, whose long blond hair whipped in the wind as he sailed through the air, leaping at an old man with black tendrils snaking out of his back. When the boy's story unfolded in Vesely's mind, he felt shaken. The boy had been kidnapped as a child. Tortured and turned into a killer. A hunter. And the world...so many people died. But then, there was hope. And sacrifice. Forgiveness. The boy's deep pain and ultimate victory nearly overwhelmed Vesely. The boy was a unique soul. Pure and trustworthy.

A woman came next, dressed in black, like a raven. She faced a man...a *dead* man, with an axe and no face. She was brave and fierce. Despite the darkness surrounding her, she found humor in the confrontation.

Vesely felt the worlds he viewed growing darker.

What is this place? He wondered, and then he decided for himself. *It's a hub between universes. Infinite universes, where anything is possible.*

The discovery confirmed his theory about why the sunken city of Atlantis was so hard to find. It was never on his Earth. It was on another Earth. The refugees from that far advanced civilization hadn't just fled across continents, they had fled between worlds and through time.

Vesely felt a coldness, more in his thoughts than his physical body. He saw a world so twisted, disfigured and consumed by death that he had to look away before he was scarred by it.

Survivor, he thought at the bell. *Take me to Survivor.*

The sound of birds and the smell of warm swirling air greeted them upon their reappearance.

"Where are we now?" Pasha asked, looking at their surroundings. They stood in the backyard of a house that was surrounded on the sides by trees. To their backs was a lake, sparkling in the sunlight.

"New Hampshire," Vesely replied. "Our time. Just minutes after our disappearance in Egypt. Home belongs to—"

"Ahem," came a deep male voice.

Cowboy spun around to find a shotgun leveled at his face.

"Mind telling me why I have a Nazi bell parked in my backyard?" Lincoln Miller tilted his head to the side, looking at Vesely around the length of his shotgun. Miller was dressed for fishing. He glanced at Vesely's chest. "Already lost the Mark 23, too, huh?"

"Survivor!" Vesely shouted, grappling Miller in a hug, as the shotgun lowered.

When Miller slapped Vesely on the back, making the man flinch in pain, he pulled away and looked his friend up and down. "You look like shit. Safe to assume you found what you were looking for in Tanis?"

"And more." Vesely stepped aside revealing Pasha and Hugo.

"As excited as I am to meet you," Pasha said to Miller. "I could really use an ambulance."

"Secret Service is already on the way," Miller said. "You triggered more than a few alarms. Adler is in the safe room with Arwen. They'll be glad to see you, but..." He glanced at the bell. "...this is a problem."

"Is *big* problem," Vesely said. "Is original bell from which Nazis stole design. Is unimaginably dangerous."

"I gathered that from your sudden appearance on my lawn." Miller stepped up to the bell, looking it over.

"Is this seriously Lincoln Miller?" Hugo asked.

Miller just grinned at him. He was used to the attention. "It won't be long before we can't keep this between us." He looked up at the tree, lush with Spring leaves, leaning over them. Vesely knew he was checking to see if eyes in the sky could see them. As the man who saved the human race, Lincoln Miller wasn't only a celebrity, he was also a target. As such, he was protected by Secret Service and one of the most sophisticated alarm systems in the world. And when those alarms went off, the troops came running and satellites turned in his direction.

The lake house once belonged to Dr. Aldric Huber, a former World War II Nazi and the grandfather of Elizabeth Adler, who had helped defeat the modern day Nazis at Dulce, and who had moved in with Miller and young Arwen. The house was deemed the perfect location, because New Hampshirites are a naturally private people, and Huber had managed to hide at the home for decades without being discovered.

Miller was the only non-president to get the full presidential treatment. The fact that there weren't a dozen agents surrounding him now was only because he insisted on privacy and the fact that the former Navy SEAL and NCIS agent could handle himself.

The chop of an approaching helicopter fueled Vesely's decision. "I have idea."

He reached into his pocket, pulled out a business card and a pen. He quickly scrawled a note, licked the backside and slapped it against the bell, where it stuck. He placed his hands on the bell's palm prints and instantly felt the connection. "Get back. Far away!"

While Miller and Hugo helped Pasha move away from the bell, Vesely closed his eyes and focused. He pictured the place, and the person, and then, using the memories implanted in his mind, he chose the perfect time. The bell began to hum. The sound grew louder even after Vesely yanked away his hands and ran for cover.

As he reached a fallen tree where the others had taken shelter, he prepared to dive to safety, but Miller held up his hand. "You're good."

Vesely skidded to a stop and turned around.

The bell was gone.

"Where did it go?" Hugo asked.

"I sent away. Far away." Vesely looked to the grass where the bell had sat just a moment ago. "To one person I knew I could trust, who can hide it from world."

A helicopter tore past overhead.

Vesely relaxed, and that simple act returned all of his pain with a vengeance. He sat against a tree trunk with a groan. "Now we get ambulance."

Miller lifted his phone, speaking in hushed tones. When he lowered it, he said, "Medevac will be here in five minutes. They can take all three of you. You can brief me after you're patched up, unless..." Miller gave Vesely a look that translated to something like, *Unless there are still bad guys that need shooting.*

"We are good," Vesely said. "For now."

Pasha placed her hand on Vesely's shoulder. "Thank you, Milos. For everything."

Vesely tilted his Stetson down and tapped the brim with his index finger. "Is nothing."

"Is something," Pasha argued. "How'd you do it?" She looked at Miller. "He just killed fifty plus Nazis, uncovered the secret of Atlantis, traveled through time—"

Miller coughed. "What? Traveled through time? Are you serious?"

Vesely shrugged. "Was bell. Could do...anything."

Miller shook his head. "Geez."

"Answer is simple," Vesely said with a grin. "I—"

"He is Cowboy," Miller said, impersonating the Czech accent. "Is gunslinger. And the very best of us." Miller offered his hand, and Vesely took it with a smile. "And if I know my Czech friend, he's just getting started."

EPILOGUE

I wake knowing that something is wrong. Something has changed. I can sense it, though I can't technically smell, see, taste, touch or hear anything different. That's not how it works. I just know.

Proceeding with caution, I slide out of bed and glance out the window. The sun pokes up over the horizon, lighting the green jungle far below. The first scents of breakfast are drifting up from the kitchen, three floors below.

Years of practice and bare feet allow me to cross the room in silence, allowing my wife to continue sleeping. She's notoriously grumpy early in the morning, so I would prefer she slept. If I need her aid, slumber will not slow her much.

I stop by the door and retrieve my weapon. Holding its weight in my hands reminds me that it's been some time since I wielded it, since I fought for my life or for anything else. *I've missed you, friend,* I think, and I reach for the door handle.

The door creaks as it opens, causing me to cringe. I wait for a sudden attack, and when none comes, I look back. My wife stirs, but remains asleep. With the door open just wide enough to squeeze through, I enter the living chamber on the other side, beyond which is the throne room. But my journey ends here.

Sitting at the center of the living chamber is a large, bell-shaped object, but more squat, almost like a UFO. It's certainly something constructed by the modern world, beyond my borders, but what it is and how it got here, I have no idea.

I search the room for danger, and finding none, I circle the device. It's covered with etchings I don't recognize—not from the modern world or from the underground. If I had seen it before, I would remember it. I remember everything.

A white rectangle slides free and falls to the floor. Bending slowly, wary of my surroundings, I pick up the stiff paper. A business card, I realize, observing its telltale shape and size.

A quickly scrawled, handwritten note is on the blank side. I read it aloud, "Is very dangerous. Does not belong in physical world. Sorry about placement."

The door behind me creaks loudly. I spin around, Whipsnap at the ready. It's a flexible shaft bearing a spear tip on one end and a spiked mace on the other. It's been a while since I held the weapon like this...ready to strike.

Kainda is there, woken from her slumber, battle hammer in hand. Seeing no danger but me, which is to say, none, she lowers her weapon and looks at the strange device. "Solomon, what is it?"

"I'm not sure," I say, but I decide to trust whoever delivered it to me. The energy flowing from the device is not from Antarctica. I don't think it's even from this world. And that it was given to me, the one person who can remove it from the physical realm and into Tartarus, reveals that whoever delivered it, had the best of intentions. Tartarus, a prison for an ancient evil known as Nephil, leader of the Nephilim, the gate to which is hidden miles beneath the surface of Antarctica, would make the perfect place to hide just about anything. It's a soul crushing place to which only I am able to travel. Once this device is there, only I would be able to retrieve it.

"Who brought it here?" Kainda asks.

I turn the card over. In raised black ink is a single word that fills up the entire card, revealing that this isn't a business card at all, but a calling card. Using my supernatural connection to the land and atmosphere of Antarctica, including everything created from it, I open the side wall of the living chamber with a thought. The stone obeys my will, peeling away. A gaping hole reveals my kingdom—the continent of Antarctica, thawed and reborn as a tropical paradise, now known as Antarktos. Next, I summon the wind, generating a tightly confined cyclone. The bell-shaped object lifts into the air. As it slides out of my tower and over the hole I've opened in the ground far below, leading to the gates of Tartarus, I read the single word aloud, "Cowboy."

A Note from the Author

—What the heck was up with that epilogue?—

If you're a long-time reader of my books, a few items near the end of this story, including the entire epilogue, might have had you cheering or smiling fiendishly (like I was while writing it). If you haven't read many of my books (or none before this), you might have been confused. If so, I'm here to explain.

When Vesely finds himself at a hub between universes, he catches glimpses of several other worlds and the characters in them. Each of the worlds he sees and experiences are books of mine. The first, with the 300-foot tall monster is PROJECT NEMESIS. The second, with a team of five facing off against a stone monster is THRESHOLD and the characters were the Chess Team. Next, he watched Solomon Ull Vincent's progress through all five of THE LAST HUNTER books, collectively known as the Antarktos Saga. And last was the feisty and funny zombie-killing Jane Harper, who appears in THE SENTINEL and THE RAVEN, written under my Jeremy Bishop pen name. Effectively, the hub that Vesely entered was *my mind*. My imagination. And I had a lot of fun writing it that way.

As for the epilogue, I have been asked countless times (I literally lost count) to write a crossover novel bridging multiple book universes. Something like the Marvel/DC crossovers. These requests led to an epilogue where Milos Vesely loosely communicates with Solomon Ull Vincent AND we get another peek at Solomon's life, post-Last Hunter. I listen to the fans! And while it is not a full-fledged crossover, it has created the potential for one. That doesn't mean it's *going* to happen. It would be complicated, to say the least, and it runs the risk of being cheesy. But the groundwork is there.

So there you have it. I hope you enjoyed I AM COWBOY, and please take a few minutes to post a review for the book. Each and every one helps new readers find my books, because the more reviews that are written, the more Amazon, B&N and others recommend them. And the more books I sell, the more I get to write! And if you're like a literary Christopher Walken, and you want "More Cowboy!" then make sure to say so. I'm listening.

— *Jeremy Robinson*

ABOUT THE AUTHOR

JEREMY ROBINSON is the bestselling author of more than thirty novels and novellas including ISLAND 731, SECONDWORLD, and the Jack Sigler series including PULSE, INSTINCT, THRESHOLD and RAGNAROK. Robinson is also known as the #1 Amazon.com horror writer, Jeremy Bishop, author of THE SENTINEL and the controversial novel, TORMENT. His novels have been translated into eleven languages. He lives in New Hampshire with his wife and three children.

Visit him online at JeremyRobinsonOnline.com

COMING IN 2013
FROM JEREMY ROBINSON

JACK SIGLER and the CHESS TEAM are back with *PRIME*, a prequel revealing the team's beginning, and *OMEGA*, what might be the final book in the series! To stay up to date on these and other releases, sign up for the newsletter at www.jeremyrobinsononline.com.

CPSIA information can be obtained
at www.ICGtesting.com
Printed in the USA
BVHW070417191020
591038BV00007B/815

9 780988 672529